TO CATCH A Nazi

KENNETH MARKEL

TO CATCH A Nazi

CHANGING LIVES PRESS

 CHANGING LIVES PRESS
P.O. Box 140189
Howard Beach, NY 11414
www.changinglivespress.com

Library of Congress Cataloging-in-Publication Data is available
through the Library of Congress.

ISBN-13: 978-0-98621-641-1

Cover and Interior design: Gary A. Rosenberg

Printed in the United States of America

10   9   8   7   6   5   4   3   2   1

*"Whenever they burn books,
sooner or later they will
burn human beings too."*

—HEINRICH HEINE (BEFORE 1850)

I. BERLIN, 1933

It was eight days since I last saw my mother. My teacher, Mrs. Preisinger, told me to report to the schoolmaster's office after the bell. When the bell sounded, I swung my book-bag over my shoulder, ran down the hall.

Two tall blonde-haired men in black uniforms and shiny black boots stood in the schoolmaster's room, caps in hand. Each had a pistol strapped to his belt. "These men want to have a few words with you, Wilhelm," Dr. Sternberg said.

"Do you know who we are?" one of the men asked.

"You're soldiers," I answered.

Not a hint of a smile creased their blank faces. I'd seen men like them from a window as they marched on *Unter den Linden*, torches held so high they burned holes in the night sky.

"Look mama," I said, "isn't it wonderful?" My mother didn't think it was wonderful, but the spectacle of the torchlight parade remained vivid in my mind. Soldiers marching, jackboots, black helmets emblazoned with a symbol called a swastika, and the steady cadence of drums as the goose-stepping soldiers approached the *Brandenburger Tor* where a reviewing stand was set up to honor the new chancellor.

"These men are investigating the whereabouts of your mother," the schoolmaster, a man with close-cropped gray hair, said, "Be truthful when you answer their questions." I had always been truthful and wondered why Dr. Sternberg felt the need to impress this upon me. Dr. Sternberg made announcements in assembly, but seldom observed the students in our classroom studies. As the soldiers and I left his office the schoolmaster clicked his heels, bowed.

Walking down the front steps of the school with the two soldiers on either side of me, I saw a black car parked outside, another man in uniform behind the wheel. Several boys from my class were watching. I thought myself special that soldiers came to my school to help me find my mother. I held my head erect and got in. I sat in the back-seat of the car between the soldiers. One offered me candy, which I politely declined.

They knew about my mother, that she was a journalist for the *Vossische Zeitung,* but now worked at Rieber's Tobacco Shop. "Where do you think she might be?" the friendlier one asked. I didn't answer. The soldier continued rhetorically, "She hasn't come for you in more than a week, has she? What if she never comes home?"

I thought, she'll come home, who else will tell me stories about my father? I remembered the night the new chancellor was elected. I could still hear the sound of the drum in my ears. That night I watched from a window, glimpsed a man standing on a terrace saluting the crowd below who loudly cheered him. I ran to my bed, got under the covers. Once again, I asked my mother about my father. By not telling me very much, she made me want to know more. On that night, instead of reading me a story, she told me about my father.

"We know about your father," the less friendly soldier said.

"He was very brave," I replied. "I will also be brave when I'm twenty."

"Would you give up your life for the Fuehrer?"

"I'm only nine years old."

The car slowed. I turned my head. Mallard ducks paraded in single file, nibbled at the weeds along the River Spree before joining a row of swans.

The friendly one asked me if I'd like to visit the zoo. The *Tiergarten* was my favorite place in all Berlin.

"Can we see the big cats?"

"We'll see," the less friendly one said. When we got to the zoo, the friendly one took out a package of gumdrops from his pocket and asked, "Are you sure you don't want even one, Willy?" I had a red gumdrop. "Take more. Go on." I had another. Finally, the friendly one gave me the whole package. I put them in my pocket.

As we walked, I ate gumdrops. It was very casual, the way two uncles might walk in the park with a favorite nephew. Before reaching the cages where they kept the 'big cats,' the less friendly one said, "We know a lot about your mother." I kept chewing. "Has she stayed away before?"

I shook my head. "She reads to me most every night."

"About *Karl der Grosse?*"

"About my father, he's had many adventures."

It was ten years since my father, Ernst Mannheim, boarded a train to Munich and never returned. "What does my father look like?" I asked.

My mother didn't answer. I pulled at her arm. "Careful, you'll tear my dress," she said, returning from her daydream.

"I'm sorry, mama."

"It's all right, Willy." She looked at me...saw I was growing up. "Your father was a long-distance runner. He wanted to represent Germany in the 1924 Olympics in Paris. He was tall, blond, with blue eyes...like you."

Freda, my mother, didn't go any further. I wasn't sure why she stopped. Maybe, it was because it was getting late and I had school the next day. Later, I found out that she didn't know the whole story herself, where my father was captured or how he died. I once overheard her say to my grandmother: "Maybe, Anton could use me. I still have a good figure." I watched as her hands passed lightly over her breasts.

"Could you do us a big favor?" The friendly soldier asked.

I was beginning to think soldiers were like ordinary people that their uniforms were for show, to make them look bigger and stronger than they really were. "Tell us, where does your mother go on her day off?"

"She goes shopping or she visits Grandpa Isaac and Grandma Sarah."

We had reached the place where the tigers were kept. One of the tigers yawned, stretched and got to his feet. He padded back and forth, snarling from time to time. I could not take my eyes off the tiger's lithe but powerful movements. I'd read or heard that Bengal tigers weighed over five hundred pounds and were ferocious.

As I drew closer to the cage, someone took my arm and twisted it.

"You're hurting my arm," I said.

"You were getting too close to the cage."

I looked up. It was the man who gave me candy, the friendly one. "We want to bring your mother home to you. Help us save her before it's too late."

"What do you want to know?"

"What was her explanation?"

"Her friend wasn't feeling well."

"Where does her friend live?"

"Can I go back to the tiger?"

"The tiger isn't going anywhere. The keeper will give him his dinner very soon."

I put my hand into my pocket. The package was empty. Furthermore, I sensed I was being observed. "We can watch the tiger eat his dinner if you'd like," the friendly one said, malevolently. I looked up at the sky. It was getting dark. Suddenly, I had more interest in my stomach than in the tiger.

"Can you take me to my grandparent's house?" I asked, politely, "I wouldn't want to be late for dinner."

"A boy shouldn't miss his dinner. How would you like to go to a fine restaurant?"

"Grandma Sarah said not to talk to anyone about my mother."

"Why didn't you say so?"

"I didn't know you that well."

"Now that you know us better won't you bend one little rule?"

"I'm getting hungry."

"We understand," the friendly soldier said, "Don't we, Horst?"

The other man nodded. "Soldiers are human beings too. We get hungry like everybody else."

"Can I have anything I want on the menu?"

"We'll see."

"My mother's friend's name is Heidi Baumann."

"Do you know her address?"

"No, but she lives in Potsdam."

The soldiers drove me to my grandparent's house in the *Grunewald*. The friendly one opened the door and lifted me from my seat and set me down on the stone walk. He sniffed the air and shouted, "Better hurry, your Jewish grandmother is cooking chicken soup."

As the car drove off, I turned away from the spray of diesel exhaust and the sound of laughter.

I remembered the laughter, but more importantly I remembered the words, *"Soldiers are human beings too."*

I didn't know if they found my mother, whether they arrested her. Perhaps, they only wanted to ask her a few questions.

As soon as I sat down at the table to eat my dinner I didn't feel well. "Have your soup before it gets cold, Willy," Grandma Sarah instructed. She was a large, perfumed woman with square shoulders, rouged cheeks and heavy legs. The gold teeth in her mouth made her look like a gypsy.

My grandfather was an old man with pock marked skin and eyes that needed thick glasses, a science professor who saw the world slightly out of kilter. I picked at my peas and carrots and told my grandparents about the soldiers in black uniforms that came to school and took me for a ride in their shiny car.

"Where did they take you?" my grandfather asked.

"The zoo."

"Did they ask you anything?"

"What would soldiers ask a nine year-old boy?"

My grandfather reached across the table and slapped my face. It was a hard slap. My face turned red, but I didn't cry. My grandfather said, "They must have wanted something. Tell me, what did they want?" He twisted my arm.

"Leave the boy alone, Isaac."

I pulled my arm out of my grandfather's grasp. "They heard I was the best boxer in my section," I lied. "They gave me advice how to sharpen my skills."

"Your skills are sharp enough," my grandfather replied, not fooled by my disclosure.

Once I got undressed and went to bed, I overheard my grandparents talking about how hard it was for Jews since the new chancellor took over. I knew Jewish boys had been beaten up not far from where we lived. If an older boy asked me about my background I told him that my father printed a newspaper for the Nazi Party. I never said a word about my mother.

I waited until I heard my grandparents snoring, and then dressed. I opened the window in my room. The tree closest to the house was more than an arm's length away. I thought for a moment. If I used the front door I would have to go down the stairs. It was an old house and the stairway creaked. I knew I'd get the strap for sure if I was caught.

Then, I remembered something I saw the acrobats do at *Zirkus Busch*. I opened the window as wide as I could, hopped onto the sill like a monkey. With arms extended I jumped out, caught the closest tree limb with my hands and swung myself. As I let go, I flew into the air, hit the soft ground and tumbled over. I scrambled to my feet and started running.

I'd told the soldiers the truth. I didn't know the address of the house where my mother's friend lived or how to find it. Probably, the police had been there by now. I decided to go home, thinking they'd ask my mother a few questions, then let her go and she'd come home.

The further I went the more fearful I became. Maybe, she did something stupid like saying conditions were worse since the new chancellor took over. The soldiers might have tried to scare her, make her swear not to do it again. In my excitement I ran so hard I had to stop and catch my breath. My heart beat faster than a drum. I remembered what the soldiers told me. They said, 'Run to your Jewish grandmother.' If they knew my grandmother was a Jew, then they must have known my mother and I were Jews as well.

I looked up at the sky. A half-moon peeked out from behind a cloud. The wind swirled. I turned my back, held my arms tightly to my body. The streets were empty, the lamps dark, stores shut tight. It seemed as if I was the only person alive, as if all the people in Berlin had been wiped out by an epidemic.

I remembered that we had studied epidemics at school, Cholera, Diphtheria, the Black Plague. There wasn't much further to go. I could see my house in the distance.

I kept walking. I was almost home when I saw her. She lay on the ground in the garden next to the house where we lived. When I was close I saw her torn dress, her twisted legs. There were marks all over her body, burns on her bare arms, bruises on her face, blood oozing from cuts and gouges. Nothing moved except her lips.

"Willy," she whispered.

I fell to the ground and crawled closer. My eyes filled with tears. Several dropped onto her face. She tried to smile through broken teeth, bloodied mouth, torn lips.

In a voice that was barely audible, she said, "...Kessler painting." Then, she was gone.

I didn't know what to do. I put my head on her chest. The wind howled. It felt as cold as the body my arms were wrapped around. I didn't know it then, but finding out who did this to my mother would take me far beyond what my young mind could possibly comprehend.

New York City, 2004

II. Auctioneer

It was spring, yet winter lingered, an unfeeling icy dagger. I struggled from my bed into my office. The air in the room smelled of old newspapers and filmy liquor glasses. A mug of cold coffee sat on a table. I stared at the newspapers and magazines piled on the floor, proof of a hundred false leads, not to mention the effort and cost to track those leads down.

There were times I wanted to throw the proof of my misdirected labors into the incinerator, let the yellowing bundles burn to ash. Whenever I had such thoughts I drank too much, ended up talking gibberish to strangers, convinced that whatever I might try wouldn't work, not where I lived—in a neighborhood of locked doors and hopeless dreams.

Something kept me from quitting, as if there was nothing that could replace the task I'd set my mind to accomplishing. I took my defeats like a soldier fighting a losing battle. I pushed hard, yet made no real progress. It was hard work, unannounced trips down dark alleys into pockets of degradation, vile-smelling places lacking the slimmest hope of vindication for its victims. Perhaps, the idea of a soft landing on an open field was too big a stretch. What about a man in the requisite trench coat exchanging sealed documents for gold, foreign script on fine paper, maps with arrows, and dotted lines, brief smiles on faces that disappeared into the mist? The result was the same, nothing changed.

Many times I asked myself what kept me going. Was it the paltry morsels I nibbled rat-like out of the letters I received over the years from a man who introduced himself to me as 'Uncle Kurt?' Where would I be without those tidbits? Would I have given up, stopped searching for the man who detained and tortured my mother to death? As long as I fed on tidbits of information, prescient pieces that seemed cut from the belly of better tomorrows, I held out. What I wanted was revenge. Getting lost in the push and shove would at least keep my edge.

Then as life would have it that day in April of 2004, I picked up a copy of *Time Out New York* and saw under Art Galleries that *DeGuerre's* on Madison Avenue was auctioning the works of a preeminent Bauhaus artist of the Nineteen-Twenties, an almost forgotten name, Anton Kessler. No, not forgotten. Perhaps, his paintings misplaced or not recognized as valuable.

I came into the gallery having walked a city-mile at a fast pace. Even at my age, if reason said it was too late to contemplate the future, my demeanor suggested otherwise. Some thought me in remarkable shape. I took no credit for what God gave me. As for my spirit, the glue that kept the parts together, on a very humid April afternoon I felt like a soldier who'd trained his entire life for this one mission.

The air inside was cool, but no cooler than the demeanor of the fifty or so well dressed men and women milling about eating canapés, and drinking wine. I soon found myself standing among a group of upscale types who gave the appearance of having gobbled their way up the food chain without losing their appetite.

Six paintings were hung so they had plenty of room to breathe. Prospective buyers sniffed around them like a pack of hungry wolves. It predicted what I should have known, the possibility that I might not succeed. What was it about these paintings? I looked hard, tried to see beneath the obvious. None of the six spoke to me. Perhaps, I needed to look harder, underneath the paint itself. Another possibility lurked, the 'right canvas' might have already been destroyed. I'd saved carefully over the years for this moment, but what if the money wasn't enough or I bought the wrong one? And, if by chance I found the right canvas, what feat of sorcery would be required to interpret my mother's truncated message?

The paintings were all charred along the bottom, as if they'd been snatched from a fiery demise. I was aware paintings that didn't portray the Aryan myth were burned by the Nazis and, somehow, felt the heat transfer into my body. Beads of sweat broke out on my forehead. I blotted them with my handkerchief, heard a voice call, "Welcome to *De Guerre's*. May I be of assistance?"

I turned. The woman was attractive, her scent spicy, alluring. "If you follow me I'm sure I can provide what you need," she said. I realized her remark was part of her job and designed to entice prospective clients. I provided my name and e-mail address. She gave me a card with a number on it.

The auctioneer, a broad-shouldered man with a high forehead and steady blue eyes, made his way to the podium. I found a seat. The auctioneer rapped his gavel, got immediate attention. He told everyone how lucky we were to be present at a rare sale of paintings by Anton Kessler, a man who faced the worst nightmare an artist can endure—the tyranny of what is sacred to the creative soul, the freedom to dream peacefully in his own imagination.

It was plain to see the effect his remarks had on the audience.

The auctioneer, seeing this, rode the crest of the emotional wave into a harbor of greater concern—the business of selling art. The first painting to be auctioned was a portrait of a man without legs sitting on a palette selling shoelaces. The auctioneer announced he would accept bids in increments of ten thousand or higher and opened the bidding at $10,000. Two men sallied back and forth until the bid reached $250,000.

Heart pounding, I raised my card. The auctioneer called, "I have $260,000. There was a slight pause, as those in the audience turned to get a glimpse of the new bidder. "Do I hear $270,000?" The man who began the bidding raised his card. The auctioneer glanced at me. I reluctantly shook my head. It would seem I'd come to the auction shortsighted as to how high the bids might go. In any case, I could only hope I'd have a chance to get one of the other paintings. "The Double Amputee" sold, but not to either man. A gray-haired woman in an old-fashioned print dress, who'd waited patiently, topped both men with a bid of $450,000.

The second painting was of a man in an abattoir holding a meat cleaver. He bled from several prominent veins in his arms. I took a glance around the room to see what revulsion, if any, I could find on the faces of prospective bidders, but I was soon called back to the action at hand.

The auctioneer opened the bidding at $50,000. It sold for $725,000. The third, of a cabaret dancer, one shapely leg in the air and covered with tufts of masculine hair sold to a man in a pink shirt for $860,000. Fourth was of a man in gym shorts wearing a gas mask hurdling trenches littered with dead soldiers. It garnered $790,000. The fifth painting showed street children holding empty soup bowls, their bellies distended from malnutrition. It topped out at $1, 250,000. So far all the selling prices exceeded any amount I could raise. It was going too fast. My head was spinning.

The last painting was of a zookeeper crawling on all fours inside a cage frothing at the mouth like a rabid beast. The bidding for this painting began more conservatively. At $200,000, one of the two men dropped out. It looked as though I might have a chance. I bid $210,000 and stayed with the back and forth until the price reached $260,000. By now I could barely breathe. My hope to gain at least one of the Kessler's was dashed when a man in a sheepskin coat expressed a sudden interest and took the last Kessler away from me. Scanning the room, the auctioneer's words came barreling out, "Going once, twice... sold!" It was over.

'Do I hear...?' I silently mocked, feeling the years press heavily against my chest. I slowly got to my feet. Only then did I realize everyone had left. The greedy assassins had made off with the prize—six prizes. In a childish fit I mumbled, "What right do they have when I've spent my entire life hunting them down?"

I wearily made my way to the door, until I heard someone call. It was the auctioneer. "Where are you going, if I may ask?"

"Where am I going?" I repeated rhetorically, "I'm going home."

"I'm sorry you didn't have better luck," the auctioneer said, with jabbing sincerity.

I looked closely at the man who offered condolences when condolences weren't quite in order. "Do I know you?"

The auctioneer shook his head. "Allow me to introduce myself. Carl Snyder."

"David Menard."

We shook hands. "I watched your struggle with great interest, Mr. Menard."

"It wasn't a struggle. It was a slaughter. I'm afraid I don't have that kind of money."

"Frankly, I never expected such a response."

"May I ask if you are also the owner of the gallery?"

"As a matter of fact, I am."

"Then, you must be in the mood to celebrate. I won't keep you," I said, once again starting for the door.

"What makes you think I'm so anxious to celebrate?"

I was stopped in my tracks. I turned. "You made a killing."

"Did I?"

"I underestimated my competition," I said, self-effacingly.

"There'll be other auctions."

"Not for me."

"If you're that fond of the period I think I can promise you more of the same in the not too distant future.

"Kessler's work?"

"Perhaps...There are many other fine German artists from the Twenties."

"I'm only interested in Kessler's work. Thank you, you've been very kind."

"Nonsense, come and have a drink with me. You can tell me all about your Kessler fixation."

"I'd rather cry in my own beer if you don't mind."

"Then, I'll join you," Snyder offered, good-naturedly. Not used to so much attention, I was flattered by the auctioneer's interest. The auctioneer added, "Is someone waiting for you at home?"

I thought of Aldo, my friend and self-imprisoned neighbor. It was our night to play chess. "No one," I said, not wanting to appear ungrateful.

"Come on, then. You can use a drink. So can I. Auctioneers are human beings too."

His words caught me up short. The words, '*Auctioneers are human beings too.*' I was sure I'd heard those words somewhere. Before I could respond, Snyder took my arm. As we were leaving the gallery, the auctioneer excused himself. "I'll just be a moment," he said, going into his private office. I overheard the auctioneer say, "*Dumbkopf!* Who pays the bills, you or me?" He returned so quickly, I had no time to give his words any thought.

We walked up Madison Avenue to Eighty-Sixth Street, then several blocks east until we reached Yorkville, a section of the city known to have a large German population. Snyder's favorite watering hole turned out to be a place called the *Old Deutschland.*

We were welcomed by the manager and shown to a table. When we were seated, Snyder ordered a pitcher of what he described as the best German beer in the States. I didn't ask questions and forgot for the moment how rotten I felt. The beer was quite good. Snyder poured. And, after several steins, I felt my mind drift. The conversation went in many directions, yet always came back to where it started, art and artists, more precisely, Anton Kessler.

"Was Kessler a personal friend of your family's, David?" It seemed we were now on a first name basis.

"Kessler? I don't think so. I'm an American. My mother and father were Americans. Are you an American, Carl?" I thought, Snyder would sound more German if it were Schneider. And, Carl might just as easily be Karl.

"Yes, but my father and mother were born in Germany."

"I thought so; so were mine."

"I thought you just said..."

"My step-mother and step-father are Americans."

"Are they alive?"

"Which ones?"

15

We both laughed.

"My father is still alive," Snyder revealed.

"Both my fathers are dead and my mothers as well."

"How old are you?"

"Almost eighty."

"You don't look almost eighty. You look my age or maybe a few years older."

We laughed heartily. "How old are you?" I asked.

"Sixty-one."

"You look younger."

More laughter! I liked the feeling, as though screws had loosened in my head and chest. Snyder poured the last of the beer and motioned for the waitress. "Let's have another pitcher of the same, shall we?" In profile Carl Snyder reminded me of men I saw when walking with my mother on Kurfürstendamm as a boy— wide jaws, thin mouths, narrow noses, passionate nostrils and fiery eyes.

"I think I've had enough," I said.

"You think too much."

The waitress came to the table to ask if we wanted another round. Snyder gave her a pinch and said, "Put it on my tab." He reached into his pocket, took out his billfold and gave the waitress a crisp twenty-dollar bill. On our way out of the bar he said, "I'll tell you something in strict confidence." He drew me closer. "The ones who bought Kessler's paintings aren't art lovers. They're lovers of themselves. Their vanity is such that they're already practicing their speeches on how they found a treasure as valuable and obscure as a Kessler, a man who painted in very vivid terms against his oppressors at a time when it was politically incorrect."

The air outside was fresh and clear. We walked toward Park

Avenue. Snyder stopped to grab a cab. Before getting in he said, "Can I drop you someplace, my friend?"

I was taken aback. Surely, the use of the words, 'my friend' were less serious than the literal meaning implied. I couldn't put my finger on it, but there was something that bothered me about Carl Snyder. It seemed like he had a motive other than the one he was taking pains to put forth.

"Thanks," I said, "I'll walk."

That night in bed, I couldn't sleep. I tossed and turned. What was it about Carl Snyder that got under my skin? He was German. Sometimes that was enough. Not in this case. He was open and friendly—*gemütlich.*

Perhaps, it was unfair to assume that generations growing up since the end of the Second World War would imitate their forbearers. It was 2004. Germany wasn't marching these days, but for what reason? Had they grown tired of the old songs or were they merely waiting for a new version to spur them into action? Were they off the Hitler bandwagon or ready at a moment's notice to climb aboard when the time was right?

I remembered things a boy of nine could never forget, the words the Gestapo used to trick me into telling them where they might find my mother. Words I would never forget. But, no words could describe how I felt when I heard the auctioneer say, *"Auctioneers are human beings too."*

III. BOOKBINDER

On a fog-shrouded dock in Hamburg, wearing a camel's hair coat a size too small, I nervously asked my grandparents, "What will happen to me?"

Grandma Sarah reassured me that two of Dr. Adler's former students would be on a pier in Boston harbor waiting for me. She pinned a card with my name to my coat and put a piece of chocolate in my mouth. In the confusion she forgot to tell me their names. As I made my way onto the gangplank, I turned. Lost in the shriek of the ship's whistle, Grandma Sarah called, "Erich and Paula Menard are your new mother and father."

For seven turbulent days at sea I wandered the deck of the ship. From time to time things would come to me about my mother, stories she told me. When the ship docked the Menard's found me shivering like a puppy dog. They rubbed my hands, wrapped me in a blanket. They tried out their rusty German on me and had a good laugh as they drove me to my new home. In the years to come, the Menard's gave me everything a growing boy needed. I could do no less than return their kindness by taking their surname and combining it with my more American sounding middle name. I was no longer Wilhelm Mannheim, but David Menard.

At eighteen, I enrolled at Boston College. By then, I'd almost forgotten the promise I made. Then, one day in the library I came upon a book featuring the work of artists of the Bauhaus period. Anton Kessler's name was prominently mentioned. But, it wasn't the artist or the period that captured my fancy. It was how the book felt in my hands. Following graduation, I told my parents of my desire to seek a new life that might provide communion with people from my past.

At the train station, my mother's eyes grew tearful. I kissed her affectionately on her cheek. When she was able to speak she said: "Don't let them impress you into their navy." It was a reference to a story by Herman Melville and apt. She and my father had raised me with good Christian values, but one thing they'd forgotten to teach me was how to take things in stride.

On a train bound for New York City I picked up a discarded copy of the *New York Times.* It provided temporary diversion until I saw an ad in the help wanted section for a bookbinder. Though I had no experience, once off the train, I rushed to the address listed. The owner of the store, a stocky man named Gruber, liked my enthusiasm and hired me on the spot.

With machines making viable inroads, binders had become an endangered species. Work proved my salvation. I had the necessary tools—strong hands, the ability to maintain concentration and an eye for the unusual. Gruber told friends he never had such a promising apprentice. In 1953, I opened a small shop of my own. In time, I developed an exclusive clientele willing to pay extra to see the past made grander—the history of their family bound in soft leather: memorabilia, photographs, and personal letters.

Nights found me restless, drawn to the smoke and sound coming from neighborhood saloons. I'd sit at the bar drinking beer and whiskey not remembering half the screwy things I did or said. I exuded something that attracted women with a history of involvement with the wrong kind of men. I never was able to figure it out. They listened to my mad ravings and didn't back away. Instead, they invited me into their beds. Invariably, dawn would bring shattering screams to my eardrums, which sent me onto the street looking for sounds to drown out the one reverberating inside my head.

1968 was a year of turmoil in the United States, two major assassinations, one racist, Martin Luther King, Jr., the other political, Robert F. Kennedy. A war in Indo-China divided a proud nation. The first letter came from Uncle Kurt that year. It was postmarked Berlin, Germany and mailed to my parent's address in Massachusetts and forwarded to me.

The letter began, Dear Willy, I am your Uncle Kurt. Your father, Ernst, was my older brother. The Mannheim family was a wonderful family, before two bloody wars took their toll. Your grandfather Gustav died in the First World War, and then your father's disappearance in 1923, seven months before you were born. Your Aunt Lotte, a beautiful child with hair like spun gold, succumbed from the aftereffects of malnutrition. Your Uncle Hans died of influenza at age twelve. Grandmother Hilda—we affectionately called her *Mut*—lived on *Kurfürstendamm* in the same flat where we grew up. After many years of poor health, she joined the others. I survive, perhaps, for no other reason than to tell you their story.

You are fortunate to be out of Germany. There is much activity here and great plans for the future, but we are a divided country and have a long way to go.

I would like you to know who I am before this centuries rain washes away the faint impressions of my life. If nothing else it will tell you of the existence of someone who never stopped caring or thinking about you. The Hitler years were not easy. When will people realize war damages both sides that no one, no side wins?

Except for you and a few friends the people I love are dead, buried in the vast underworld of our European graveyard. I tread the streets and countryside lightly for fear of rousing dead spirits, my ghost-like perambulation in deference to those whose lives were sacrificed. I have written because I want to know the last living male Mannheim, to connect my mortality to the future. I want to share with you what I remember of your father and mother and welcome reading whatever you might be willing to share with me. Your long lost and often misdirected—Uncle Kurt

The letter was handwritten in English on fine quality paper. The content of the letter, for all its sincerity, seemed cryptic, written by an intelligent man with deeply held feelings. Meanwhile, I'd been unable to find out anymore about Kessler and lived in limbo, wrestling with a tenacious past that wouldn't let go.

The letter renewed my determination. It also evened the playing field, each of us needing something from the other. With new resolve, I wrote of the work I did without mentioning my part in my mother's capture or of my solemn oath. Instead, I asked questions, about things I could only imagine before the letter arrived.

There was a joyous tone to the next letter I received despite the rather grim story it told. It spoke of 1923, the inflation, piles of worthless money, starving people, the influenza pandemic and the pitiful result, death or a shameful survival—men, women and children—cutting up the remains of horses lying dead in the streets.

"Your father rode his bicycle all over the city looking for work. He went to cafes hoping to meet someone who needed a strong young man looking for a job. Having no luck, he consoled himself playing chess. Even at twenty, Ernst was a remarkable chess player, winning games from anyone foolish enough to play against him.

I wrote back asking my uncle if he remembered any of the player's names, that there was interest in the United States connected to Weimar Germany, that I was binding a book for a man writing about those very times. It was a lie, but not a very big lie. In truth I had bound a book for someone who discovered a photograph album filled with snap-shots of his parent's life in Germany through those years.

The reply came quickly, There were many players. The Romanische Café was a gathering place for intellectuals—writers, musicians, actors and artists. Anyone who was anyone might be there at any hour of the day or night. In the main room intelligentsia ate soft-boiled eggs and drank coffee. The place was noisy, smoke-filled with many conversations going on at once. Ernst played chess in a small room where silence was mandatory.

There was always a group of onlookers, players waiting to get a glimpse of this *wunderkind* who was willing to take on all comers. Your mother was usually there to lend her support. On occasion well-known figures appeared. Bruno Schneider, who played chess with Ernst when they were boys and now a man of considerable wealth, showed up one day in a strange outfit, a long-sleeved blouse and a skirt suggesting a less masculine side.

One man in particular took his losses to your father rather hard. Freda Adler, not yet your mother, was amused by his mannerisms, the way he fastidiously folded his red handkerchief into peaks and put it into the breast pocket of his suit jacket or gnawed on a toothpick until the day he nearly choked. Freda laughed out loud and his face turned as red as his handkerchief.

Resigned to the fact that Ernst was too good for him he brought his sketchpad and charcoals. The game no longer interested him. Freda was all his eyes required—that and what he could do with her with his art. He caught her in many moods as she watched each chess battle unfold. On occasion she exhibited the pained intensity of a woman in love. Another time she affected the pose of pensive observer. Young as she was, at nineteen, she wrote a column for the *Vossische Zeitung*. The artist sketched her with soft lips parted, as she watched your father with a sensuous blend of awe and desire.

The artist's name was Anton Kessler. His drawings captured your mother in ineffable poses so skillful that anyone who saw them was convinced of his genius. Rather than have a showing of his work, the artist became political, painted surrealistically. He became famous, but as is usually the case, for all the wrong reasons. I hope I have been of some help, Uncle Kurt.

* * *

Mid-week, drinking to excess, sleeping fitfully, I vaguely recalled an order someone placed and dragged myself to my desk. I waded through a pile of papers looking for the invoice—without success. I couldn't remember when the job was due, only that it was an expensive job requiring my complete attention—the binding of a thin volume of poetry with Moroccan leather. Could my memory be failing? I felt myself sinking, drowning, a nine year old boy weighed down by his refusal to countermand his solemn promise.

The phone rang. I picked it up with a hand that, for some reason felt swollen closing around the receiver. It was Carl Snyder. He asked me if I'd care to join him, his wife and some people from the auction.

"What people?"

"Naturally, the winners. I never invite the losers. However, in your case I'll make an exception," Snyder said, with a nimble humor he used mainly for his own amusement.

"Don't fuck with me, Carl." There was no answer at the other end. I was sure I'd gone too far. "Forgive me. I haven't been sleeping well," I said, adding, "Tell me where and when and I'll be happy to attend."

Despite my initial response, Snyder gave me the address and particulars. He lived on Fifth Avenue, several blocks from the Metropolitan. The get-together was on Sunday afternoon at two.

I put the phone down, looked at my hands in amazement. They opened and closed as if lubricated with Marvel Mystery Oil. Could the mind restore paralyzed hands by renewing a demoralized soul? Could a person change his appearance without plastic surgery? Intelligent people accepted dents in the physical machinery of friends to tap deeper into places where the power switch could be turned on. Though I wouldn't consider him a friend, the electrician in this case was Carl Snyder. His telephone call provided me with a shred of hope. Naturally, I was anxious to find out what his motives were.

I went for a walk. The air outside was damp, the sky gray. Trees, whose narrow branches starved for color a few short months ago, were turning green. A gust of wind forced me to turn away from the pulverized macadam. Snyder said his father was alive. It brought to mind a story my mother told me about my father, one I never forgot.

It went something like this, "On my way home from a piano lesson a young man darted out of a building. He ran so fast the raindrops seemed to bounce off him like water from the hood of a taxi. He crossed the street. I knew in another moment he'd be gone, that I'd never see him again. He stumbled. My heart leaped in my chest. I ran to him—through a crowd of people. By then, he was back on his feet. I asked him if he was all right. He said he had a cramp in his stomach. I looked at his narrow waist and said, "What stomach?" He looked at me with a deep intensity, as though I'd touched a part of his inner being that no one else had ever been able to reach. He said, "Has anyone ever told you how pretty you are?"

"Not with their eyes wet with tears," she said.

* * *

On Sunday I got up early, ate breakfast, showered and dressed. I put on a freshly pressed pair of gray pants and yellow turtleneck. Before leaving the house, I strapped on a shoulder holster, put a pistol into the holster, my arms into a blue corduroy jacket and seeing no bulge when I looked at myself in the hall mirror, removed my eyeglasses.

I thought, my close vision was better without glasses. I needed close vision. I needed to see things the way a child sees them, or rather the way a child doesn't fail to see them.

I reached Snyder's place on time only to find I was first to arrive. Carl introduced me to his wife, Trudi. She was a good-looking woman in her late-fifties, big-breasted and blonde. She was the kind of woman who fit snuggly into the world Carl Snyder provided.

Speaking with a slight Spanish accent, she asked if I'd like something to drink. Not wanting to give the impression I drank this early, I said, "Whatever you're having." Trudi smiled, then excused herself and left the room.

"All she drinks is mineral water," Carl explained.

"She needn't bother on my account."

"No bother. Louis will fix whatever you want. So glad you could come," Carl said, rubbing his hands together, large, meaty hands with pink palms.

"Mineral water will do fine. Did I get the time wrong?"

"Go ahead, sit down. Relax."

I sat down on the sofa, my attire in sharp contrast to the pristine white leather. Louis, a curly-haired man of Spanish descent, served me Vichy water with a slice of lime, clicked his heels and left. He wore a two-piece black outfit that had the same effect as a uniform.

"Nice place you have," I said, sipping my drink, looking around. The faint strains of a Beethoven sonata could be heard coming from another room. Carl Snyder followed my eyes. "I've some nice Scandinavian pieces, if you're into Scandinavian pieces."

There was a playful manner to the way Carl Snyder spoke, one with which I wasn't secure. It made me feel like Cary Grant in a house full of German spies. What was wrong with the plot of this drama was I had no soon-to-arrive companion as beautiful and loyal as Ingrid Bergman to help me catch the criminals.

The sound of voices could be heard in advance of a cluster of high-spirited women. They strode into the room, voices brimming with interest. The men, shorter in size, briefer in words, brought up the rear. The group soon filled the living room with their perfume, name-designer clothes, perfectly coiffed hairdos and polished shoes.

Carl Snyder got up to greet his guests. They acted as if they were friends before the auction. One thing was certain. The newcomers had something in common: possession of one of the extant Kessler's.

Feeling outnumbered and badly positioned, I got to my feet.

Ordinarily I would by now have found some item of interest, perhaps a book to glance at or a piece of sculpture to caress, anything to make myself appear less conspicuous. This was different. I had the oddest feeling I was close to finding my mother's murderer.

I recognized several people from the auction, forced a smile or two and waited patiently. I relied more on patience these days, once I discovered age made patience a valuable commodity. I had the nicest little clump of liverwurst slathered on a bed of lettuce atop a stale cracker and replaced my mineral water with straight whiskey. I was about to take a sip when a woman threw me a smile. I'd become used to that sort of smile from younger women and took it with no more seriousness than had I been compared to a movie star.

The smiling lady was smartly dressed in a tailored black suit with skirt to the knee. She had unbelievable legs and got her money's worth on the rest. She was a blonde by choice though I had a feeling there'd be evidence she was once a little blonde girl, and used to receiving lots of attention. I guessed her age to be about forty. She wore her jacket open. A loose-fitting blouse created the sort of chest activity that immediately engaged my interest. I'd avoided this kind of woman all my life, until now.

I wandered to the fireside mantel over which was a portrait of a man who looked to be of the new breed of contemporary German leaders. I turned and the woman threw me another smile. Like many women born after the Second World War she did what she pleased. Women of this kind would stalk a man with an elephant gun if they had a mind. This one drew up alongside me like I was a tugboat and she the 'Queen Mary.' "What took you so long?" I asked.

"Once I get on cruise control I sometimes lose my bearings."

"When I get on cruise I just keep going."

"Too bad…Just when we were getting to know each other."

"My name is James Bond," I said, offering my hand.

"Cat Woman," the woman replied, taking my hand. "I'm not usually attracted to older fictional detectives."

"Nor I to cats."

"You have such nice hands."

"How can you tell?"

"You use them a lot, don't you? In any case they're warm."

I smiled, took my hand back, feeling as though I passed the hernia exam for my army physical. I wasn't sure why, but the lady seemed interested. "Nice-looking too," she purred.

"I'll bet you say that to all the older fictional detectives you meet."

"Only ones I might be inclined to know better."

"So! What do we have here?" Trudi inquired, stepping on a provocative line. She'd been watching. "You've been dominating Mr. Menard long enough, Ilse."

Trudi put out her arm, which I took gallantly. Ilse pursed her lips. I had the feeling she wasn't going anywhere—at least not without saying goodbye.

"There are people Carl thinks you ought to meet," Trudi whispered.

"Who are they?"

The words were barely out of my mouth when we came upon a man and a woman in animated conversation. The two were at a point where they needed someone to help them settle a difference of opinion.

The woman, a bosomy, middle-aged battering ram in a red velvet gown, asked me what I thought about the lack of creative genius in the world. A narrowly built, bearded man in a dark suit broke in to prod me, offering a choice, "Is the gene-pool slipping or is it merely a condition evolving out of world-wide greed?"

A third person, a slender man dressed in a one-piece jumpsuit, something as close to a new color as I'd ever seen, a blue that might be violet to someone or green to someone else, smiled, turning his tanned face into a fisherman's net of wrinkles. "Are you sure I'm the right person to ask just because I happen to be standing here? I might as well be waiting for a taxi for all I care about mindless chit-chat," he said with a thick European accent.

I nodded politely, turned to the other two and said, "Would it trouble you if I joined the gentleman waiting for a taxi?"

The bearded man, full of jowls and jelly stains on his tie, engaged the woman's flaccid arm in his leaner version, and off they went, he snatching the last of the liverwurst as it was on its way back to the kitchen.

The man standing next to me looked to be a man in his eighties and a smoker. I knew all the signs, having lived with parents both of whom were smokers. Yellow teeth, brown upper lip, gray pallor—I didn't need an alarm clock when I lived at home. The wrenching sound of my mother's cough woke me at seven every morning. Erich and Paula Menard died in their seventies, Erich of lung cancer at seventy-one, Paula of congestive heart failure at seventy-four.

"Thank you for bailing me out," I said.

"Don't mention it," the man answered.

I noticed that the man had hardly touched his schnapps and said, "Looks like neither of us are drinking."

"Perhaps, we have other vices."

"Perhaps."

"A man without vices is like an oven without fire."

"My name is David Menard," I said, extending my hand.

"Alex Berg," the man said, taking my hand, adding, "Are you one of the chosen few?"

"I beg your pardon," I said, not loosening my grip.

"I didn't mean to offend you. I only meant to ask whether you were one of the winners in the Kessler sweepstakes."

"I wasn't that lucky," I said, releasing Alex Berg's hand.

"Too bad."

I took another look at the man standing next to me. Surely, work had been done on the man's skin. Not the vanity-cuttings of an expensive plastic surgeon, but lifesaving skin grafts. Any show of emotion—smile or frown—caused wrinkles to form. I was sure he'd been badly burned.

"Tell me something," Berg said, breaking my concentration, "Do you always stare at people?"

"Sorry. At my age my eyes tend to be lazy."

"You seem about as lazy as a big cat lying in the sun. Let me guess. You're a year away from retirement—government work isn't it?"

"I'm not the retiring type."

"Are you sixty?"

"I'll be eighty this June."

"Impossible. Who did your face?"

"My father and mother, a long time ago."

"Perhaps, the man with the hair on his face was on to something, about the gene-pool slipping. Can you guess how old I am?"

"I've never been good at guessing games."

"You wouldn't believe it anyway."

By now, the party was breaking up. Drinkers were being steadied and pointed to the door. One could hear the sound of rattling keys, heartfelt goodbyes and kisses that vanished into air thick with the smell of alcohol, stale food and entropy. I looked around for Ilse. She'd gone. I shrugged. I'd made two forays. Neither led anywhere. There was a little time, as stragglers made trips to the bathroom, or looked for lost companions.

"If I were you, sir," I said, "I'd give up smoking. You'll live a lot longer." Alex Berg chuckled, but made no attempt to pursue the conversation. Louis brought him his cane and accompanied him to the door. I wandered down the hallway pretending to browse, my eyes darting everywhere until they fastened on a room whose door was ajar. I nudged it open with my elbow.

Drapes blocked the natural light. I could see a large bed, several paintings. One looked like the portrait of a woman. Without glasses and at the present distance, in dim light, I couldn't quite make it out. I was about to move closer when I had the feeling there was someone behind me. "Are you missing something, sir?"

"The bathroom, if you'd be so kind."

"You passed it on your stroll," Louis explained.

Walking as if I needed eyeglasses, I found the bathroom, disappeared for several minutes. When I came out Louis was waiting to guide me should I get lost again. Carl Snyder was at the bar having a martini. "I struck out," I reported.

"Don't be so hard on yourself, David."

"You can call me David only if you allow me to call you Carl."

"I like your dry sense of humor, David."

"Since the mutual admiration society picnic, wasn't it?"

"Don't you mean the 'printer picnic'?"

"What?"

"Excuse me," Snyder said, going off to speak to Louis.

The words 'printer picnic' gave me a start, jarring my memory enough to shake the family tree. What fell out was the knowledge that my paternal grandfather, Gustav, was a printer before the First World War, that my father, Ernst Mannheim, printed a paper for the Nazi Party in Berlin. And, there was more. When Carl Snyder returned, I asked, "What was that about some kind of picnic?"

"It's just an expression. Some families have secret whistles. In my family the men tell stories about the good old days...over and over."

His words were like ice picks chipping at my resolve. The only way Carl Snyder's father could know a story like that, the same story passed down from my paternal grandmother to my Uncle Kurt to me, was if he'd been told about the picnics by a member of his family, or as seemed more likely that he heard it from his father.

Snyder remained sanguine; I pretended disappointment, but not so serious a disappointment as to suggest the stakes were any higher than they'd been all along. I'd won the auctioneer's friendship by maintaining a sense of humor despite things not working out in my favor. I thought it prudent to maintain the pose.

With that Trudi, who'd been instructing the servants, came over and asked: "How did you make out with the Frankmans?"

"Were they the ones?"

Trudi nodded. "Each bought one of the Kessler's." I looked puzzled. Trudi explained. "They're married in name only. They live apart...catch up at parties and social events. Were they helpful?" I shook my head. "That's too bad."

I was about to leave when Trudi said, "My sister asked me to give you this." I visibly brightened, as Trudi handed me a slip of paper with Ilse's phone number.

IV. ILSE VAN NESS

The sun disappeared behind the art museum, its pink luminescence gradually fading into a sea of gray. The city took on the anonymity that was both its charm and its foreboding. I didn't dare look back, but walked quickly, breathing the sick-sweet spring air, not allowing a single thought to slow me down—not yet!

Before I knew it I was in Chinatown. Rather than turn around and go home, I found my favorite Chinese restaurant. It was one of those without ornamentation or fancy lighting and paper tablecloths. Coming inside, I was greeted warmly by the owner and shown to a table. The clock on the wall read 9:45 PM, late for dinner. Used to the uneven hours of city-people, the owner understood. As for me, I'd spent a good deal of my life eating at strange hours, alone, a long dark shadow on the back wall of some out of the way place.

The waiter brought fried noodles, a pot of tea and condiments…took my order. Dipping a stale noodle into a small bowl of mustard, I thought my perseverance might be rewarded, but only if I could supply the shadow on the wall with enough sustenance before it began to fade. Of course seeking someone who, if he were alive, had to be at least a hundred years old conjured up the self-possessed image of a madman. Still, I wouldn't let go.

The age of the man had no meaning. Finding him was what mattered.

I felt warm and opened my jacket, reached inside and let my hand rest on the holster holding the loaded revolver. I'd practiced my marksmanship for many years in a deserted warehouse on the upper West Side and no longer doubted my willingness and ability to use the weapon. Only I was warm. The reason, it punched holes in my specious argument that warmth was proof of an efficient circulatory system. More likely, it suggested the threat of danger looming.

In removing my hand, the slip of paper Trudi gave me fell to the floor. I reached down, picked it up. It provided Ilse's address and cell phone number in the West Village. Waiting for my dinner to arrive I brought the note to my nose. It had a faint scent of perfume. After a plate of Chinese vegetables and rice, I sipped my tea and read my fortune, "You will meet a tall dark stranger." I smiled at the unreliable prophecy.

I was about to tear the note in two when the waiter came by and poured more tea. I sipped the tea slowly, wondering if meeting Ilse was one last rub of my nose in the knowledge of what I'd missed all these years…a turn of the knife in a body covered with invisible scars. It was almost 11:00 PM when I called. She answered on the second ring.

"You took your sweet time. I'm practically in bed." She was acting as though we'd been friends forever. Still, it was a turn-on.

"I sometimes think of food. Can you forgive me?"

"I could make us something. Not all modern women are paralyzed in the kitchen."

"With such fire you might burn the soufflé." The laughter at the other end was genuine and music to my ears. "What about lunch, tomorrow?"

"How about dessert…now?"

"Be there in ten minutes."

"Meet you downstairs."

My taxi arrived as Ilse locked the downstairs door. I paid the driver, waited for her to cross the street. "Are you in the mood for anything in particular?" I asked.

"There's a little cafe not far from here."

"Shall we walk?" Ilse nodded, slipping her hands into her coat pockets. She looked different without makeup and high fashion . . . graceful, relaxed.

"How do you know Carl?" she asked, casually.

"I met him at the gallery."

"Ah, yes, *De Guerre's.* Did you buy anything?"

"I did my best." I said, with open hands.

"The Kessler Auction, of course!"

"Are you familiar with his work?"

"The Bauhaus period in Germany, wasn't it…Nineteen-Twenties?"

"I'm impressed."

"Trudi is the real artist in the family. I saw you admiring her work."

"Was that Trudi's?" Ilse nodded. "And, what do you do?"

"I work for Kyle Charlton of 'Charlton Chats.' I'm his amanuensis."

"I watch his show religiously. I admire his courage."

"Everyone thinks Kyle's got a big set of balls."

"What do you think?"

"I know better," Ilse said, without shame, "Where are you from?"

"Germany. I came to the States when I was nine."

"Are you retired?"

"I'm a bookbinder."

"I was right about your hands. They need to be strong, don't they?"

"Machines handle most of the work these days."

We'd reached our destination, a small café painted the colors of New Mexico. We ordered coffee and for the next hour talked about any number of things politics, religion, philosophy, even sports. It was quite painless and in some ways priceless.

Walking back to Ilse's apartment there was less conversation, more sidelong glances and sweet smiles. "What is it a converted brownstone?" I said, looking up at the stone facade.

"Why don't you come and see for yourself?"

Why not indeed? As she unlocked the front door, I stood behind her, inhaling the sweetness of her. I followed her up one flight of stairs. She had the top floor, five or six rooms, large kitchen, two baths. Nice views. Not bad for a working girl. I was about to take off my jacket, when I realized I was packing a gun.

"I'll just be a moment," she called.

Before sitting down, I took a look around. There was a hall closet. "Take off your jacket and make yourself comfortable." Again, she called. I was doing just that when she returned.

"You didn't have to freshen up on my account," I said, "This is about the time I start to wilt."

"Stop trying to be clever. You passed the entry exam with flying colors."

I sat down in a chair across from Ilse. She wore silk pajamas. I picked up a book sitting on a table, looked at the title: *"The Rise and Fall of the Roman Empire."*

"I thought you'd be interested in more modern history," I said, placing the book on the floor next to the lamp.

She found a book with less prolixity and brought it to me, "Here's one you might enjoy, *'The Eight Pieces of Brocade.'*"

I took the book, flipped through the pages. I was puzzled by its content.

"It's Qi Gong, what some Chinese do when they wake up," she explained.

"I thought the Chinese were Americanized. You know: skip morning sex and ablutions, eat breakfast at McDonald's."

Again, Ilse laughed. "Is there no reaching you?"

"How old are you, Ilse?"

"I'm forty-nine."

"Are you?"

"I am. You have any problems with that?"

"None."

"How do you spell that?" she asked, lightly brushing off earlier religious training.

I laughed. "All right, so I'm not old enough to be your grandfather."

Since I had no intention of staying the night, I made no effort to further that direction. Ilse, too, was self-contained. I didn't mind Ilse's self-containment keeping me at a distance, felt no need for schoolboy heroics. It kept me alert, while preserving my own detachment. The technique worked before, older man allowing the animal attraction women found appealing in him to move things further along. I sensed there was a need in Ilse beyond what may have begun as a favor to Carl—agreeing to find out what she could about me and report back. I waited for her to make the first move.

Looking at Ilse sitting on the floor with her legs curled up under her like a schoolgirl, I sensed she wanted more than token payment for extracting whatever information I might be willing to offer. I saw it in her eyes, faint smiles that came and went like soft summer breezes. Questions I had to ponder, What did I want from her? And, could I keep her—as I had with the others—out of my heart?

The lonely wood where I made my home kept me on a path consistent to my sworn oath. Having come this far, noting the twisted passion of Anton Kessler, I wondered what last-minute reprieve saved the painter's grotesque creations from a fiery demise, and what might save me—now!

Ilse padded across the rug on all fours like a cat. I leaned forward. She put her head on my thigh. I stroked her silken mane. She removed a clasp; let her hair fall over my knees, her face hidden in a sweet-smelling waterfall of hair. I moved my legs apart.

I'd been in this position before, but former tactics no longer seemed useful. Suddenly, I had no desire to draw back, to wait for a moment of my own choosing. Something real was happening. The question was whether I could regroup. But, once the balloons inside me filled to perfect balance I lost myself in the moment.

In bed, we disrobed quickly without words.

"What were you like as a boy?" She stopped herself. "I know what you were like."

"How do you know?"

"You were in my fondest dreams."

"Black and white or Technicolor?"

"Don't you believe me?"

"Not a word."

She put her fingers to my mouth. "You have no idea what you do to me."

I turned toward Ilse, with the weariness of someone who'd spent most of his life playing bedroom games, games that lessened the burden of a search for someone I couldn't find. I kissed her tenderly on the lips. She accepted the kiss as down payment on a night of kisses. Her kisses were sweet, no alcoholic aftertaste or mint-flavor of the squeeze tube. It was the sort of good taste God endowed to women who bore no grudge against the 'Isle of Man.' Her lips were warm. I got into the game by charting a course of my own.

It was like no other time I'd ever known—no time I'd be able to duplicate. What mattered most was the way she responded to each tender touch. I was what I'd always been—someone on a mission to find the man who tortured my mother in ways I couldn't imagine until I spent that night with Ilse, and realized my feelings for one woman could be duplicated and felt for another.

I did my best to seal the tiny cracks with kisses, tried to calm my mind, only to have it jump the track. Not in the direction of love, but somewhere in the more discreet countryside of doubt. I caught her looking at me.

"Tired, 'Big Cat'?"

I shrugged.

"Long day?"

"Long life."

"Something wrong with that?"

She snuggled close like a tame house cat. I thought it strange that both of us reached this place at the same time, behaving as if our ship could survive any storm, willing to sail on to wherever the sea dropped off all the drawn maps.

Despite the uncertainty in her eyes she was mine. This I knew. More disturbing was the fact that I might belong to her as well. I saw no way around this bump in the road. I was lying beside the woman I always wanted, a soft-breathing, sweet-lipped, tender-touching creature, who managed to silence the sounds in my ears and bring soft light into my eyes.

V. The House of Schneider

I reached out, my hand brushing against the pillow. My eyes opened. There was a note next to the house keys. It read: "David, There's plenty to eat in the fridge. Help yourself. If you'd like fresh rolls there's a bakery around the corner. Kyle has a surprise guest on tonight's show. The staff doesn't know who it is. I could fix us something to eat, if you're in the mood for a late-supper. Ciao!" Ilse ????

She left a fresh towel for me at the foot of the bed. I showered, dressed and went out. The sweet aroma of the bakery was enticing. I bought two seeded rolls and a cheese Danish and then returned to Ilse's apartment. The mailman, a young man in his twenties, was about to put Ilse's mail into her box when he saw me take out the door key. He looked me over, then handed me the mail without a word said between us.

On my way to the kitchen, I passed a French door with its shade pulled down. I tried to see inside, but the shade blocked my view. I glanced at the mail instead. An envelope postmarked Argentina had the quality of fine paper, the texture of which I was familiar. All I could make of the envelope was that Ilse's name and her address had been written by someone, most likely a man and foreign-born, with poor handwriting.

After breakfast, I listened to my voice mail and read Ilse's note again. It was sweet. She was sweet. But, it was Monday after all. I had things to do, not the least a dinner engagement with Aldo and a home cooked meal. I crumpled the note and dropped it into the trash basket under the sink. I'd make a counter offer. Tuesday night dinner at an intimate restaurant and whatever came after.

Bright sunlight poured through a kitchen window momentarily blinding me. Shadows long as goal posts pointed the way down the carpeted hallway. My interest in what might lie behind the French door was rekindled. I tried the door. It was locked. There was a skeleton key on the ring. I tried it, and it worked.

The room gave one the feeling of going back in time: heavy maroon drapes of velvet, hand-crafted oak bookcases filled with volumes one would expect to find in a musty legal library. The portrait of a man hung on the wall over a large desk. He had gray hair, neatly parted, wore a dark business suit, a white shirt and striped tie. There was an air of prosperity about him, someone whose life offered challenges that were never met with anything less than a serious-minded attention to detail. He projected a demeanor that gave one the feeling that nothing could get to him in the same way they got to lesser men, men like me who protest the difficulty they find getting the results they expect and yet unwilling to yield their uncertain position on the long way home.

It wasn't an unattractive face: blue eyes well spaced, nose patrician, cheeks full, thin lips mild and well mannered. He wore gold spectacles, the glass part larger than any I'd ever seen. He was obviously a man who seldom lost control, who maintained order and discipline in his affairs. The artist brought this out with some skill. I came closer, my eyes straining to read the artist's name scrawled in the lower right corner, but hard as I tried I couldn't decipher it.

Walking home, I tried to make sense of what I'd seen. For

example, the portrait could be Ilse's father. Or, it could be a former lover. There was more, but for the moment it eluded me.

Back home, I unlocked the left bottom drawer of my desk, removed Uncle Kurt's letters. I ran my fingers lightly over the envelopes. They had the same feel of the letter mailed to Ilse from Argentina. Carl Snyder's remark about the 'printer picnics' sent me leafing through the letters until I found the one I wanted.

I read with great interest: No matter how Fritz and Rudy feel with regard to stealing from a Jew Herr Dietrich said stole from other people, I feel ashamed of breaking into the man's apartment, standing by while Rudy works himself up into a sweaty rage, before Fritz hits the man over the head with the base of an iron lamp. Walking home, my pockets bulging with loaves of bread, cheese, fresh fruit and tinned fish—I'm so hungry I take a banana, peel it and stuff it into my mouth. It's like a pebble dropped into a shallow pool of water. I take a second banana. No matter how hard I try, I can't stop thinking about my disgrace and gorge myself by stuffing another banana into my mouth.

How can I pretend to be proud of what I've done? How can I pretend nothing happened? I remind myself that bringing home food for my mother, my two brothers and for my sister, who are slowly starving to death, is worth any sacrifice. All I have to do is look at Lotte—she's eleven and tall for her age—see her blue eyes shine out of their bony sockets. At last I reach the place where we live. And, puke my half-digested dinner into the street.

Mut is sound asleep in a soft chair in the living room, her mouth slightly agape, legs hanging over the armrest. Her dress is raised just above the knee, legs bent like a half folded chair. There is the faint aroma of her sex. It occurs to me that while *Mut* is a widow she is a relatively young woman. I watch her labored breathing and think, how many solutions is she working out in her dreams? How many solutions has she rejected for fear of choosing the wrong one? Rather than wake her I decide not to tell her where I've been until the next day. It will give me time to think of better lies.

Mut grew up on a farm in Freising, a small town in Bavaria known for its brewery college. Her father and mother were farmers and Catholic. From descriptions of her life, I weave a picture in my mind of how she and her family live from day to day. They rely on skills learned over generations and find simple pleasure in their work. It is done with a joyous spirit because they're accepting of their way of life and because over time it builds a solid foundation of family.

I wonder if people still maintain the old ways in towns like Freising. Not much remains of the life I knew as a boy growing up in Berlin. Each day reminds me that survival depends on a willingness to do terrible things. I go into the kitchen and unload the food from my pockets. There's no ice in the icebox. Nevertheless, I put the perishables inside, leave the tinned goods and apples on the table and go to bed.

The following morning I'm awakened by the sound of a door being slammed. My heart beats fast. I jump out of bed thinking what if the police have caught Fritz and Rudy and are coming for me? I walk into the living room in my underwear, my hands clenched. *Mut* looks at me. "It was Ernst," *Mut* says, "He went out to look for work."

I go back to my room feeling I showed poor judgment the night before. How can I hire myself as a card-carrying goon of some sub-human culture whose fists are for hire? What possesses me to go with those two maniacs—Fritz and Rudy? And, who gives Otto Dietrich the right to decide who lives and who dies?

Mut is ironing in the kitchen. I don't know how long she

slept, what time she finally went to bed. I sit down at the table and peel an orange.

"The children were so good," *Mut* says, dipping her hand into a bowl of water, dousing the shirt before laying on the heavy flat iron. The hissing steam sends up a sweet-sour smell of soap and sweat. "They washed and dressed and when they saw the food, they thanked God, shared an apple, ate some cheese and washed it down with two gulps of water. Then, they thanked me. Can you imagine? I told them: "Thank your brother, Kurt. He brought enough food for everyone. They went to school like little lambs." Then, without looking up from her ironing, she asked where the food came from.

I watch *Mut's* eyes grow larger. They are seeing too much. It's like waiting for a train that's late. You know that a train was due, yet you keep looking, as if looking will make the train get there sooner. I suffer from the same disease of waiting, wanting, not knowing. Perhaps, it's the result of seeing too much, a seeing filled to the brim with sights that defy belief and are best forgotten. When I don't answer right away, *Mut* says, "I waited for you to come home." Her eyes are red with deep, dark circles. I say, "I didn't have the heart to wake you."

Mut tells me that Ernst met a man last night at the *Turnverein* who wants to change things. She asks me if I know anything about this man. I tell her he speaks for the worker's party, that his name is Otto Dietrich. She asks, "Who are they? Will they help people like us?" I don't answer. She asks about Herr Vogel. I lie. I say that he told me I was his best rent collector...that he's going to give me a raise. Another lie! She says Herr Vogel is a selfish man who thinks only about his wife and his daughters. If she only knew I'd already lost my job, that Herr Vogel is dead. *Mut* finishes ironing my shirt. The collar is frayed, but it's clean and without a crease. She asks if I want to wear it to work so I put it on.

Mut asks if I remember from when I was a young boy. I say I remember holding her hand crossing streets. She asks if I remember picnics in the *Grunewald.* Papa called it an excursion, but she said it felt more like an explosion of food and beer, all that male energy running around in the woods. I tell her that I remember running in relay races, eating *apfelstruhdel* and watching Ernst play chess with Bruno Schneider.

"His father, Herr Schneider was a big flatterer." She blushed. "He loved my *apfelstruhdel.* And, how!" Herr Schneider owned the biggest printing establishment in Berlin, 'The House of Schneider.' He published a newspaper and pamphlets of the latest scientific discoveries. He was killed in the war—same like your father."

I put the letter down and drew back in my chair. What better proof was there of a connection between Carl Snyder and ghosts from the past than the 'printer picnics?' And, what can top the arrogance of a man who has the audacity to merely change his name from Schneider to Snyder and go on doing whatever he pleased, believing he could snub his nose at the world and get away with it?

Once more, I picked up the letter and read: Bruno Schneider was a year older, but my brother won the match. My father wanted Ernst to go to the university. He said Ernst had a good brain and might be a scientist or a doctor someday. I have enclosed a photograph. Though faded and torn in several places, it shows Ernst raising a trophy over his head and Bruno Schneider draping his arm around his shoulder. My father took the picture. He could have asked Herr Schneider to put the picture in his newspaper, but he wanted Ernst to concentrate on schoolwork. He said: First education, then chess.

VI. CHARLTON CHATS

mong my books, newspapers, and magazines, I sometimes felt like a boy at play in a bathtub filled with wooden boats. But, grown men don't play with boats in bathtubs. They're more inclined to set chessmen on a coffee-table and let the war begin, a war fought with black and white replicas of worthy ancestors who gave their lives in brave struggles that lifted them high into the air—until they came down to earth.

There was a knock at the door. I recognized the sound and called, "It's open, Aldo."

Aldo Antonucci, a pudgy, pale-faced chemist in his late-forties, wearing a ratty-looking blue bathrobe, came into the room on spindly legs. A mountain of lava-like hair piled high on his head made him look like he was part of a Slovenian juggling act.

Aldo's parents were hard-working immigrants from Italy, descendants of farmers from Parma and shoemakers from Milan. When Aldo's marriage ended in divorce, the shame his father felt was so great that Aldo, his only son, was no longer welcome in his house. Aldo had no choice but to live alone in a city where many people lived alone unless they had a pet. I supposed that I was Aldo's 'pet person' and worthy opponent in the chess games we played each week.

Aldo was a good player when he wasn't suffering from brain-fog, a condition caused by the medications he took to help him forget how his life turned out. There were antihistamines he took for his allergies, steroidal nose-drops he took for lingering bronchitis, sleeping pills he took when he bombarded himself with thoughts of how he took too many things for granted during his failed marriage.

I checked my watch. It was just past three. "You're early."

"I didn't hear you come in last night."

"I didn't come in last night."

"You shouldn't be shacking up with bimbos at your age."

"What's my age got to do with it?"

"Don't mind me. When I get tired of hammering myself I seek other prey."

I enjoyed Aldo's self-deprecating humor. "I may go out tonight," I said, casually.

"It's game night."

"We could grab a bite and start early."

"Suits me."

"You have any sauce left?"

Aldo grinned. "Do I have any sauce? Give me a minute, I'll be right back with something Picasso would have saluted."

As soon as the door closed, even with visions of Picasso in red sauce, I closed my eyes and drifted off. In what seemed like minutes Aldo returned and placed the sauce on the stove, then put water up to boil in a large pot. The smell soon brought me around.

"Catching up on your sleep?"

"I wasn't sleeping. I was dreaming, or something."

Yes, or something! Something was going on. Was it a steady downpour, a river of rising doubt, crossed wires, electricity sparking revelations? What was it, David Menard—or should that be, Willy

Mannheim? Were you beginning to see contradictions? Sometimes when Uncle Kurt referred to himself it seemed as though he was someone else. But, who was he, friend or foe? Was Carl Snyder's remark about the 'printer picnics' an innocent slip of the tongue or does he suspect something? And, was Ilse's interest and availability part of a well-conceived plan designed to do you in?

The sound of my cell phone rose from the sofa like music from a miniature merry-go-round. I walked and talked while Aldo babied his sauce.

"I've never seen a broadcast of a television show before. I'd love to come. Soon! Ciao!"

"Sorry, Aldo, I have to go."

"At least have a bite," Aldo pleaded.

I weakened—at least my taste buds did. The aroma was intoxicating. I had a small plate of stuffed shells, a glass of red wine. "We'll finish the game tomorrow," I promised. Aldo raised his glass as I left and called, *"Salute!"*

I floated onto the street. To add to my delight it was the kind of mild, breezy city day that provided a wide avenue to stretch my legs.

Crossing to the glassier side of Broadway, I entered the Dunbar Building, showed my ID to the concierge and received a pass Ilse had left for me. I took the elevator to the seventeenth floor. Ilse spotted me, walked down the hallway, the sound of her heels like castanets. "Glad you could make it," she said, kissing me on the cheek. She had on a smartly tailored navy blue suit and a pale green silk blouse. *Tres chic!"*

"Are we allowed to talk?" I asked, looking around as Ilse led me into her office.

"We can see and hear the show from here. I take notes, so we can't chit-chat once the show is on." I looked around. The studio was about what you'd expect: wires, cameras, paraphernalia.

"When does the show begin?" I asked, as I entered her office. Ilse looked at the clock on the wall, then at her Swiss-made wristwatch and said. "We go on the air in exactly eleven minutes."

"Is there a…?"

"Down the hall and to your right."

I pushed the door leading into the men's room. There was a row of urinals. I went to the first one, noticed another man standing further down. When I glanced up I had the feeling I knew the man from somewhere. By the time I was through the man had left.

I walked back to where I left Ilse, but she was now on the other side of the glass talking to Kyle Charlton. Charlton appeared younger and thinner in person. The man I glimpsed taking a pee was flipping through his notes. Technicians lit up like fireflies. One could feel palpable tension with electricity in the air.

By the time Ilse returned, the show was due to go on in five minutes. Ilse threw me a smile. I smiled back. I turned my attention to Kyle Charlton's guest. His face still looked familiar— an apple-cheeked man with hair worn long in the style of the Sixties. I refocused on Kyle Charlton. Seated at a polished mahogany table, Charlton affected what had become his trademark-expression. a look suggesting an insatiable craving for books, the puffiness around his eyes visible proof of a sleep-deprived man.

Controversy being a hallmark of the show, what audiences tuned in to watch, Charlton was never in a hurry to apply a tourniquet to stop the bleeding if the discussion became heated. He would provide a safe landing field, but only if his guest earned it by warding off Charlton's buzzing squadron of attack-planes with élan.

"My guest this evening, Marty Sunshine, is someone many Americans know," Charlton began, "War hero, author of the best-selling book, *One World,* he's taught at UCLA, The University of Chicago, Harvard and Columbia. He's also lectured on behalf of the *One World* organization he helped co-found and which I know he'll be delighted to fill us in on. Welcome, Marty to 'Charlton Chats.'"

"Thank you, Kyle."

"I'd like to begin by asking you whether it bothers you that some people see you as being somewhat of an oddball."

"The last time I looked this was still a free country. Everyone is entitled to an opinion."

"That's very generous."

"I don't mean to sound flip. It's just that people have a hard time reversing deeply held feelings about someone whose public persona has left a rather strong imprint, with a dossier to prove it."

"Is there a dossier?"

"When you put yourself in the way of the kind of characters I have you run the risk of setting up a game of back and forth."

"Do you mean like chess?"

"It is sort of like chess. Only the stakes are higher."

"And, what side are you on these days, Marty?"

"The winning side—of course?"

"Ours?"

"Are we winning?"

"Touché."

"All joking aside, I am optimistic about our chances what with a new man getting a shot at running a country that's been slowly dying of malnutrition of the spirit, while putting up a good front, a very soft and well-fed front I may add."

"You seem in pretty good shape."

"That's because I play squash three times a week. And, if I'm offered a ride I demur and walk."

"I wish I had the time."

"Make time, Kyle. You're worth it."

"Did you learn that sort of discipline while you were a POW?"

"I learned it long before Nam. My father was my role model."

"What kind of work did he do?"

"He sold brushes door-to-door and always had a good word for everyone."

"No question you've had a fascinating life, Marty, captured by the Viet-Cong, tortured until you told the enemy you were sent by the US government to assassinate Ho-Chi-Minh, sentenced to death by the Central Committee, sentence commuted by no one but Ho-Chi-Minh himself when you convinced the leader of the communists you'd tell the American people on national TV how you were coerced into performing the mission. Released at the end of the war in 1975, to come home and be branded as a traitor to your own people and finally, if there is a finally to anything Marty Sunshine does, admit to a stunned American audience and Vietnamese public that you lied, using a ploy advocated in ancient Chinese lore. Strange, wouldn't you say, that Ho didn't pick up on it?"

"By then they were drunk on victory. They may have gotten a little careless."

"In any case it's quite a story."

"Have you ever been put in a 'squeeze box'?"

"I'm not sure what a 'squeeze box' is."

"They give you the amount of room a boxed piece of electronic equipment has, only you stay in the box Jack, until they sound the all clear."

"It sounds rather daunting."

"Daunting? Man, you shit and piss. It just doesn't go anywhere."

Ilse's eyes opened wide. I suddenly remembered who Marty was, only his name was Brenner not Sunshine. Meanwhile, Kyle Charlton tactfully changed the subject, giving Marty a chance to tell America about *One World*.

"I vowed I'd write one last book to express on paper what I had in my heart. It took me years to complete and I had help along the way with my careless English."

"I might add, with great power."

Marty drank from a mug on the table. "Kyle, you sure have a way of making things sound larger than life. It must be your New York background."

"I grew up in Ohio."

"It doesn't matter where you're born, Kyle, since everyone knows we're all descended from the same place in Africa." He took another swig. "You do recognize the evil element at work, don't you?"

Ilse looked at me; I looked at Ilse. "What's in that mug?" I asked.

"I was about to ask you the same question," Ilse said, going off in search of the director.

"Some of my best friends are dead."

"Go on, Marty."

"I'll skip that story, if you don't mind."

"Tell me, is Sunshine your real name?"

"Now what made you go and ask a dumb question like that?"

"I get paid for asking questions—even silly ones."

The interview was winding down. After the verbal fireworks the two men passed the peace-pipe based on two major issues. Marty Sunshine's desire to sell his book and Kyle Charlton's magnanimity meant to show he was open-minded and willing to take on all comers.

"The name of the book," Kyle picked up a copy of the bulky hardcover for the close-up camera, "is *One World*. The book is written by Marty Sunshine. I've read it and recommend it to anyone seeking a better understanding of the human condition as told by a man who has spent most of his life doing just that."

"Thank you, Kyle."

Kyle turned for his close-up. "Tomorrow night my guest will be 'Mario the Magnificent,' latest in the Houdini-marathon of escape artists. Mario will tell us about his plunge to the bottom of the canal in Venice locked in a bank safe with a combination only the bank president himself knows. Skeptical, frankly, so am I! Until next time..."

Coming off the stage set, Kyle Charlton showed no aftereffects of the interview. In fact he had a look on his face that suggested it was all in good fun. Ilse used the opportunity to introduce me to Charlton. "Ky, I'd like you to meet a friend of mine. David Menard, Kyle Charlton."

"Nice to meet you, David."

"Nice to meet you, Mr. Charlton." We shook hands. Charlton was about fifty, not as imposing as I thought.

"Call me, 'Ky.' How did you enjoy the show?"

"I liked it very much."

"David's a big fan."

Marty Sunshine, who detoured for a return trip to the john, joined the group.

There was a moment's hesitation, then one of recognition. "How are you these days, Mr. Menard?" Sunshine asked.

"Not so bad," I replied, "Good to see you've put together another book."

"What other book?" Charlton asked.

"Ky reads a book a day," Ilse revealed.

"Skim-reads," Charlton corrected.

"I didn't write it. It was a family history in photographs. Mr. Menard did most of the work. His professionalism brought a great deal of joy...especially to my father."

"When was that?" Charlton asked.

"Before I went to Indo-China," Sunshine said. The playfulness he exhibited in front of the camera was toned down, his mood sober.

"I'd like to have a look at it sometime."

"I'm afraid there's only one copy."

"You're putting me on."

"David's a bookbinder, Ky," Ilse revealed, taking some pleasure in making the fact known.

"By hand," Sunshine said, adding, "One of the finest in his field. He did me the honor of preserving something I still treasure." Sunshine looked at his watch. "I really must scoot. I'm due at the embassy eight sharp."

"Say hello to Jason Randolph for me. We're old friends."

"Not the American embassy." There was an uncomfortable moment of silence. "The German embassy," Sunshine said, smartly clicking his heels before leaving.

"I can't believe it," Charlton said.

"That's putting it mildly," Ilse added.

"How long have you known Marty, David?" Charlton asked.

"He came to my shop back in the mid-Sixties."

"That's forty years ago."

"I suppose it is."

"Would you care to join me for a drink?"

"Not tonight, Ky. I'm making dinner for David."

"You're a lucky man, David."

I took a long look at Ilse, "That I am."

There wasn't much conversation in the elevator or on the street. To me it felt like the old cat and mouse game. Ilse had made me her 'Big Cat,' no doubt using the term to play up to my male ego. More likely I was the mouse who sensed he'd better watch out for conveniently opened packages of cheese standing in my path.

We decided to walk. The city seemed impartial to those who sought its pleasure by offering an assortment of distractions: a phantasmagorical array of lights, colors and sounds; high-powered vehicles speeding toward destinations to the cacophony of horns and sirens.

"Quite a coincidence," Ilse said, leaving room for an explanation.

"I knew his face, but couldn't place it."

"Sometimes when it takes longer it's nice."

"Last night?"

"Yes, last night."

"It's late to bother making something to eat, don't you think?"

"I only said that so we could be alone. Unless you prefer drinking with Ky?"

"I'd rather answer your questions than his."

"What makes you think I have questions?"

The traffic light was against us. We stopped at the corner. "Is it the sex that interests you?" I said, sorry as soon as the words passed my lips.

"Do you really think that?" There was a catch in Ilse's voice. I did my best not to let her reaction bother me.

"I'm a big girl."

"We don't know much about each other, do we?"

The light changed. We walked on. "What would you like to know?"

"Who was your favorite teacher?"

"My father. Who was yours?"

"My mother."

"Was she pretty?"

"I don't know…maybe"

"My father was a good man," she said, resisting the temptation to elaborate. She seemed to be holding her breath, doing her best to quell the emotion filling her chest. I saw but wouldn't allow myself to feel. Was Ilse falling in love with me or was she playing me? There was too much at stake to take chances.

"What's Carl Snyder to you?"

Ilse's chest released the air she'd been holding. "What a silly question? He's my brother-in-law."

"I meant beyond the family connection."

"What are you after, David?"

I avoided a direct answer by looking up at the sky and saying in a mild tone, "When I was a boy I was amazed at how magical the world seemed. I was this tiny speck on the enormous face of the universe—nothing more. There were times when I thought I might catch a glimpse of God when his back was turned."

"You sound like someone riding a white horse."

"How can anyone judge another person's passion?"

"I don't have to judge. I know," Ilse said, taking my arm, snuggling close. She was warm and seemed happy. Still, I wondered how much of her attentiveness was real, how much based on loyalty to Carl.

It was nine by the time we reached her place. The pace of the city receded, replaced by an uneasy calm, one with which the city-dweller was on intimate terms. I looked around, saw the emptiness behind the dark windows, no give in the asphalt and felt caught in the silent undertow.

Ilse opened the door. Her nails were an inch longer than mine, painted a military blue-gray. Once inside, I followed her up the stairs.

"Getting Marty Sunshine to appear was a real coup for Ky. I guess he didn't tell anyone because he was afraid of a leak."

"Does that happen often?"

"It happens. You must be starving," she said, as we reached the top of the stairs. She took off her jacket. "I'm hot," she said, the top buttons of her blouse open.

"I know."

She shook her head, then opened the door.

"I'd settle for a good night's sleep."

"Is my 'Big Cat' sleepy?" Ilse's lips formed into a soft pout. I grabbed her around the waist, pulled her close. "Easy," she said. I kissed her. I took her hand and guided her into the bedroom. She purred in my ear like a tame housecat. Her eyes widened.

I looked at her in amazement. She looked at my young-old face with tender expectation as only a young face could and reached inside her blouse, unhooked her bra. There in the magical wonderland of a dark bedroom two people, doomed from the onset, somehow managed to invent a language of love all their own.

In the afterglow, lying beside one another, each of us silent within the moment, there was no sense of time or of time passing. Ilse made the first move, sliding off the bed. The flesh of her ample backside jiggled. My eyes followed every movement she made. I wondered to myself, could I keep my emotions for her at bay, and was this just a game for her?

VII. Confession

Light filtered in through a crack on one side of the opaque shade, making entry through the postern gate possible. Uncle Kurt wrote: It was a warm July evening in that fateful year of 1923. Ernst and Freda had asked me to join them for dinner. It was a special occasion, their two-month anniversary. I waited until dark, walked to the restaurant and entered by way of a side door. The police were giving me a hard time for some caper they thought I was involved in. Ernst and Freda were involved with each other. They were arguing even as I greeted them. Once again Ernst was jealous over Freda's posing for Kessler.

Ilse stood in the doorway holding a tray. She wore a bathrobe without the belt. It allowed free movement and gave me something to look at. Cerebral thought was flattened. I couldn't take my eyes off her. She'd sliced various cheeses and placed them on crackers. There was also a carafe of wine and two glasses.

I watched her pour the wine. We ate and drank ravenously until all that remained on the tray were crumbs and empty glassware.

"Are you always this talkative?" she asked.

"That was very nice."

"Yes, it was," Ilse said, letting her robe slip soundlessly to the floor.

She lay down next to me, wriggled her body until her head was on the pillow beside mine. "It was quite a coincidence, you knowing Marty Sunshine."

I wanted to turn off the cat and mouse stuff, tell her the truth. For one thing: Marty Sunshine's real name was Martin Brennermann. He and his family came to the US from Germany. Instead, I wondered what secrets Ilse had locked inside her head.

"Are you that good?"

"Don't you know?"

"I meant your work."

"Come see for yourself."

"I'd love to," she said, like a young actress playing up to the director for a chance at a choice role. "When can I come?"

"Anytime," I said, sliding my hand under the covers until it found a slit in the underbrush, felt her body come alive.

The following morning, after breakfast, in the bathroom, I saw a calendar I hadn't noticed. Returning to the kitchen, I had a smile on my face.

Ilse, who'd been straightening up saw the look and asked, "What's so amusing?"

"I've never seen a calendar of nude men before."

"Very simple: when I don't have such an ardent lover, I masturbate."

"When are 'you girls' going to stop trying to be like men?"

"On the day 'you boys' start treating us like women."

"I had that coming. I'd never treat you as anything less."

"That's what you say now."

I took a long look at Ilse and felt confronted by the catch in her throat, a few tears and the suggestion of deeper involvement.

"This James Bond doesn't always wake up bright-eyed and bushy-tailed," I said.

"I like my James Bond."

"Do you?"

"Very much." She looked at me so seriously I couldn't help but chuckle to myself, thinking: She can't mean that. She's just being playful.

"What's so funny?"

"Us."

She took my hand and led me toward the locked room.

"What's in there?"

"Someone who'd like to know whether your intentions are honorable."

Ilse unlocked the library door; we went into the musty room. Once again, I looked up at the portrait on the wall. This time I saw a somewhat different man, one with a regal tilt to his head and a nose that was more on the incline. Ilse brought me closer to the portrait. "This is my father, Stefan Van Ness."

For the time being, I respectfully went along with the charade. "He's quite good-looking. How old is he?"

"About sixty. He'll be ninety-eight in August."

"What happened in between?"

"He was murdered."

"Who was responsible?"

"What's the difference?"

"Tell me."

"He was killed by the Mossad with some assistance from the American government."

"How do you know that?"

"They left their calling card."

"Forgive me. I'm not familiar with the methods of the Israeli secret service."

"They broke into our house, surprised him in his den. There

was a struggle. He tore loose a 'Star of David' from the neck of one of the assassins before they shot him. My mother found him."

"I thought Israelis kidnap their victims, put them on trial."

"They've killed more without the benefit of a trial."

"I see."

"He wasn't SS. He wasn't Gestapo." She spoke as if the rest of the German people had no part in the war and so had no sleepless nights. "He was living out his years in peace with his wife and daughters."

"They must have had reasons. What kind of work did your father do?"

"He was a physician."

"Where was he during the war?"

"He had a private practice in Frankfurt. He told us what he did. He kept no secrets from Trudi and me."

"What kind of medicine did he practice?"

"He was a cosmetic surgeon."

I thought, a valuable occupation after the war when Nazis were trying to lose their former identities. "What father would tell his children the truth about so terrible a connection?"

"There was no terrible connection."

"I'll tell you something..." I began, breaking off before finishing.

"Go on."

"Not yet."

"Then, I'll tell you. My father is the only other man I truly loved besides you."

"Ilse, it's too soon. How can you know?"

"I'm not a child, David. I know my heart. Don't you know yours?"

The smell of old books was beginning to get to me. "Not yet," I admitted. I felt the likelihood of her father being murdered in the way she described was too improbably melodramatic, down to the 'Star of David' clutched in the victim's hand.

"How old were you when this happened?"

"I was twelve."

"Did you see any of it?"

Ilse shook her head. Did Trudi…?"

"No," Ilse broke in, "Trudi was away at school."

"Had she met Carl Snyder?"

"The Snyders were friends of the family. If it weren't for Carl and his father Trudi and I would have been left without money or a place to live. David, my father's death drove my mother insane. She's in a private asylum in Argentina. Can you guess who pays for her care?"

"Okay!" I said, feeling I'd heard enough. "Did I ever tell you that my mother was Jewish?"

"So? I'm sure Carl won't hold it against you," Ilse said patronizingly, passing over my disclosure as though Jews should be thankful for whatever the world offered them.

"How kind of him." I replied, keeping a tight rein on my emotions.

"I'll admit at first I was trying to find out things about you," she said, with light insouciance.

"Why?"

"Carl thought your interest in Kessler's work seemed too personal for you to be a serious art collector."

"What else?"

"Germans who were forced to find homes in other countries after the war tend to be a little paranoid. Can you blame them?"

"Like your father?"

"Like Jews they too have been persecuted," she offered, unaware of how odious her comparison sounded.

At that point I realized I was saying too much, that Ilse, whatever her true feelings, was still reporting to Carl Snyder. And naturally, finding out a few things more about me would make him want to know more; my connection to Kessler among others. Then, what? "Is Carl a party member?"

"I can't answer that."

"Not even to the person you profess to love?"

"Trudi is also someone I love."

"Surely, Carl wouldn't hurt his own wife?"

"Carl brought us here from Buenos Aires. He saved our lives. Trudi has studied with the finest art teachers. She's one of the best copyists in the field. Experts say you can't tell her work from the original."

"What kind of art is that?"

"She does originals too...Brilliant originals."

I thought for a moment. "Is she doing Kessler 'originals' for Carl?"

"I don't know."

"Don't you?"

"I can't hurt my sister, my very own flesh and blood."

"The Kessler's sold at auction, are they forgeries?"

"I can't say."

"Ilse!"

"And, what if they are?"

"Does Carl own any of Kessler's original work?"

"I don't know."

I looked at Ilse, placed my hands on her shoulders. Applying too much pressure would send her running back to Carl, a direction she might go in any case. I looked up at the portrait of Stefan

Van Ness, felt Ilse's eyes tracing my own. "Your father looks like a man who'd give someone the benefit of the doubt."

"He was always fair-minded."

"What if I told you there's a history between Carl's family and mine?"

"Is there?"

"My grandfather and Carl's were printers in Berlin before the First World War. Each year the two families picnicked with other printers and their families."

"How do you know?"

"My Uncle Kurt wrote and told me about them."

"If that's true, why not tell Carl? You might find you have a great deal more in common than you think."

"What if I find evidence that Carl isn't who he appears to be?"

"What evidence?"

"I need to get into Carl and Trudi's apartment without anyone finding out."

"For what reason?"

"I want to look around, see if I can find out something that might help me."

"I want to help…" Ilse said, turning away, "But you ask for the impossible."

"When I was nine I saw my mother lying in an alley, or should I say what was left of her. She'd been tortured by the Gestapo and left for dead."

Ilse's eyes grew serious. "What a terrible life it must be for you, my David…all these years?"

"Would you do any less for your father?"

Ilse shook her head. "I'm not sure what to do." She took my hand. We sat down on the sofa. "David, help me understand."

"At the party I caught a glimpse of a painting in their bedroom. Tell me, Ilse, do they have an original painted by Anton Kessler?"

"I told you..."

"This would be of a woman."

"Is she your mother?"

"I don't know."

"Do you have a photograph of her?"

I shook my head. "I left Germany with only the clothes on my back."

Ilse looked at me as if seeing me for the first time. "When I first saw you I thought, what an honest, self-effacing person."

"James Bond?"

"Our little joke," she said. Again, her face grew serious. "I remember a story my father told about the Nazis. I'm sure he wanted to spare us, yet I felt its bone-chilling effect." It was the first time Ilse showed sympathy toward the victims of Hitler's Third Reich.

"More reason to go ahead."

"Are you armed?"

"I carry a pistol."

"Do you know how to use it?"

"You'd be surprised."

"I'm afraid for you, David," Ilse said, impulsively getting to her feet. At the window, she looked out. The few trees one was able to see hadn't flowered. "Trudi is having a showing at the gallery on Saturday night. She asked if we'd like to join them."

"I could make an excuse for not being able to go."

"I couldn't do that to Trudi."

"As long as I can get into the apartment while they're out."

"I have a key."

"Fantastic."

"Louis will drive us and return to keep an eye on things. He'll wait for Carl to phone when he wants to be picked up. Louis is a martial arts type, carries several weapons. How much time would you need?"

"Just enough time to look around. I should be out of the apartment by the time everyone gets back."

"You had better be."

"I will."

"David, you're crazy to try this."

"Ilse, I've waited a long time."

"I'm going to work," Ilse said, facing me with two black eyes, tears mixed with mascara like wet soot. "Perhaps, I can do something useful there."

"Not until you wash your face."

Ilse went to the other side of the room and saw the damage in a mirror. I came up behind her and turned her around. "Be careful, I'll dirty your shirt," she said. It was too late. My lips had found hers; she responded hungrily, like someone who would never grow tired of hungry kisses.

VIII. REFINING THEIR TECHNIQUE

I clamped the book in the lying press, applied paste to the backing. My intention was to affix Uncle Kurt's letters to pages in a book. That way there'd be a permanent record. Waiting for the glue to soften, I thought about Uncle Kurt— what he said in one of his letters. Will anyone care about me when I die besides my nephew, *the last Mannheim*?

Scraping the glue with the edge of my knife it would seem my uncle felt he was running out of time. Interest and time: areas of concern for men as we grow older. How often had I deceived myself into believing that if given enough time I'd create an interest among others in my most important work? How often had my illusions come to naught? I opened the book to the middle section, cut the sewing thread stitches. It felt strange, as if I were removing stitches from a wound not quite healed

In 1989, the year the Iron Curtain was lifted, Uncle Kurt's letter arrived on time. It read: Approaching my eighty-fifth birthday, I think of my family, especially your father. How much better for you had he lived and I perished. He could tell you much more. For example, the night the three of us ate together in the Russian restaurant—I forget the name of the place—the night before he left Berlin.

Ernst isn't sure what to do with his hands so he lays them on the table. He has long fingers and wide palms. Freda puts her hands on the table too, but far enough away so she can *creep* them forward. Ernst quickly pulls his hands back. It makes him laugh. "How can you make me laugh, when I have no desire to laugh at anything?" he asks.

"Laughter is one thing that can always be trusted as a friend."

"What are some of the others?"

"There's the ability to see things as they are, not as we'd like them to be."

"Of course one must be realistic."

"Not to become *so* realistic that we miss what is spontaneous, joyful and beautiful."

"You're beautiful, Freda."

"Am I?"

"You know you are."

Freda pays him no mind. She realizes he's a little crazy. "Another is the imagination," she says, "There we can create a world of our choosing."

"You sound like a poet."

"I'm a journalist."

"Are you one-dimensional?"

"I write some poetry—bad poetry."

"I don't believe that."

"I'll show you both sometime. We can all laugh at it together."

"I would never laugh at your poems," Ernst says."

A serious attitude comes over the two of them. They look at each other with the desire and curiosity young lovers have when they want to take off each other's clothes. The food finally comes. It is a fine meal. Freda says the maître d' is also the owner and assistant chef.

"Who's the chef?" Ernst asks.

"His mother."

We all laugh. Then, we eat. It is the first decent meal we've had in some time. Ernst acts as if he doesn't want to move from the spot. The prowling wolf finally rests.

Freda's articles in the *Vossische Zeitung* sting the human conscience. They show no mercy for those who bring Germany to her knees. The inflation speaks a universal language, she writes, yet the government is mute. Its response, print more marks. It doesn't take a financial expert to figure out that by flooding the country with worthless paper the currency loses value. As prices go up the man in the street can't afford to buy the bread he needs to survive. Meanwhile, *Raffkes* like Hugo Stinnes build industrial empires on foreign currency. They are winning this desperate struggle. Despite government promises, there is no solution for workers forced to bear witness to their own family's starvation.

Leaving the cafe, Ernst reaches into his pocket, takes out the silver watch our father gave him for doing well in school. The time is three o'clock. The time is always three o'clock on our father's watch. Freda sees how hopeless his life is and her heart goes out to him. What does she see in him that moves her? Perhaps, the way his body works, all the parts in synchrony, or the way his hair falls across his forehead, stringy and matted. Or the way he laughs with tears in his eyes.

I wrote to Uncle Kurt, said he was being too hard on himself. I told him how much his letters meant to me, how I looked forward to receiving them.

Another letter, On the day my brother is arrested in Augsburg and taken into custody by the Gestapo, he soon finds out they know everything—where he's going, and for what reason. They want the names of every member of the group to which Kessler and notable others belong. They torture him. These Gestapo, new at torturing people, take the opportunity to refine their technique.

When there is no word from Ernst, Freda fearlessly boards a later train. It must pique Otto Dietrich's curiosity enough for him to send his storm troopers to provide her with an escort. The mighty monkeys have plenty of room on their dance cards. Freda, pregnant with you, is given safe passage.

Meanwhile, the Gestapo feed Ernst a steady diet of the wild goings on in Berlin. They suggest that Freda has been unfaithful. They doctor photographs to make it appear as if she's been in the company of other men. They break into her apartment while she's working. They use her typewriter, a print Ernst recognizes and knows more about because he's a printer himself. They fabricate love letters using the names of men familiar to Ernst. They show him a love letter with a broken letter v and Freda's signature, signed by an expert forger in their service.

Photographs appear at breakfast, letters to new lovers. Ernst asks about Kessler. They tell him Kessler's been replaced in his wife's favor by another. He asks, "Who is it?" Their answer: "A man who plays chess at the Romanische Café." They don't tell him his name. He asks, "Is it someone I know?" They don't answer.

* * *

Carl Snyder was too young to see what happened during the war. Since Carl made it his business to become my friend, I don't know what to expect, especially the way things stand now. Still, I was sure Carl had some knowledge of these events.

I cleaned up and returned to my office. Things seemed to be in order. However, there was a faint, but unfamiliar odor. Aldo was generally disinclined to waft anything my way but cooking aromas. This was a new scent, yet strangely redolent. Could it possibly be a woman's perfume?

I sat down at my desk, unlocked the drawer where I kept Uncle Kurt's letters. They seemed just as before. To make sure, I reached down and took them out, held them to my chest, inhaling them as I walked around the room. Whoever got into the apartment and broke into my desk were professionals. They left no marks, not so much as a faint scratch on the lock. Nothing appeared to have been taken. Still, I refused to dismiss the affair as some sort of faulty reconnaissance; set my mind to finding out more about this skillful intruder.

I replaced the letters and locked the desk drawer. The thought of them being handled by someone would not leave my mind. I called Ilse, only to find that she was in the middle of a meeting. I walked across the hall to rouse Aldo from his afternoon nap when something glittery caught my eye. I stooped down and plucked a woman's earring from the aquamarine carpet—delicate, expensive. I put the earring into my pocket as Aldo, huffing and puffing, made his way up one flight of stairs carrying an armful of packages and wearing a bracelet of shopping bags around his wrist.

"You'll never guess where I've been."

"A fire sale?"

"I've been watching a real pro at work."

"You went to Burger King for lunch."

"The 'King' part has no real meaning. Where I come from a

burger is a burger. I don't know how you feel, but they give me *acido.*"

"I'm stumped."

"I went to see a chef prepare a meal the way a meal is supposed to be prepared."

"The Culinary Institute?"

"The guy works the corner of Seventy-Second and Broadway. He put on a pretty good show until the cops came."

Aldo handed me the key to his apartment and I opened the door. He put his packages down on the kitchen table, the perishables in the fridge. Meanwhile, the worried look on my face induced Aldo to slip into his favorite role of faithful friend and compassionate listener.

"Who's this woman you've been seeing?"

"Her name is Ilse van Ness. Do you have a minute before you start dinner?"

"Sure," Aldo said, following me across the hall.

"I think someone's been here."

"What do you mean, 'here'?"

"Someone got into the apartment. They've gone through my things."

"They take anything?"

I shook my head. "How's your nose?"

Aldo felt the fleshy protuberance just above his mouth. "Not bad if you like the giant economy size."

"Never mind that. What do you smell?"

Aldo sniffed the air like a bloodhound, "Tomato sauce?"

"Want to hear something funny? I'm nine years old and I'm still playing the same game."

"Relax," Aldo said, bringing his easygoing nature out from behind the raccoon circles around his eyes. "I hope you're not referring to the noble game of chess," Aldo said, bowing his head in mock deference.

I smiled, evincing a pose central to the life the two of us had crafted for ourselves.

"Get the pieces."

"Tonight I make the best dinner you ever tasted," Aldo said, heading for the door.

A few minutes later, Ilse called. She apologized for her tardiness. I told her what happened. Her response was matter-of-fact. "I think you're exaggerating."

"I don't think they found what they were looking for," I said, leaving room for a wide avenue of surmise.

Ilse sighed. "I thought you were going to show me your work."

It sounded as if Ilse wanted to see for herself. It was hard for me not to think that whatever information she picked up in the process would be most helpful to Carl and his friends.

"I promised to play chess with Aldo tonight."

"Sounds like fun, 'Big Cat'," she purred.

"What do you know about chess?"

"You might be surprised."

"Come by in an hour."

"I'm starving."

"Don't worry about dinner. Aldo makes an amazing tortellini with broccoli rabe and endive salad."

"I wasn't thinking about dinner."

"You're bad," I growled.

I was still trying to figure out how the break-in happened when Ilse got there carrying a loaf of Italian bread and a bottle of red wine. I introduced the two people I cared about most, hoping they'd be friends. I noticed that Ilse wore heels that made her taller than Aldo. Always true to his sauce, Aldo excused himself to check on how dinner was coming along. Ilse came over and kissed me. I helped her off with her coat and pulled her into the living room.

"What is it?" She asked, caught off balance.

"Do you smell anything?"

"Male energy."

"You can do better."

"Perfume."

"Much better."

"It's not my kind."

"Whose kind might it be?"

Ilse sniffed, followed the smell into my office. She looked under my desk and said, "Nice legs."

"I like yours better."

"It's called Blue Spruce."

"Who uses it?"

"Forest Rangers."

"Ilse!"

Ilse laughed a silly little laugh. "I know of only one woman. Her name is Gisele."

"Who is she?"

"She's a freelance photographer."

"Who sent her on this mission?"

"Who do you think?"

"Now I remember; the blonde at the auction."

"It doesn't prove anything. I'm sure there are other women who use the same perfume."

"Who also happen to be photographers, who know how to get into the desk drawer where I keep Uncle Kurt's letters?"

"Maybe, Carl thinks you know something he should know."

"He could have asked me."

"Would you have told him?"

"That depends, Ilse, this isn't Nazi Germany—at least not yet."

"I wouldn't make such a big deal out of it."

"I can't believe you're defending him."

"Isn't it time for you let go of your obsession? Next thing your liable to say is the whole thing is a conspiracy." Ilse laughed again. I clenched my fists. "Go on, hit me. You'd like to, wouldn't you?"

"No, Ilse, I wouldn't."

"Is it because I tell you things you don't want to hear?" I touched Ilse's face. She bit the soft side of my hand—hard. Aldo called from the kitchen, "Hey, you guys dinner is served."

Ilse excused herself and went into the bathroom to freshen up. I paced. If Gisele photographed the letters, as it seemed she had, then Carl knew the Mannheim family a lot better. Ilse returned. Seated at the small table, the three of us devoured what Aldo insisted was just a little something he threw together. When dinner was over, Ilse volunteered to wash the dishes. Aldo, a glass of wine nearly at his lips, said, "Go inside." Ilse saw Aldo look toward the living room as if the chessboard was beckoning. She removed her shoes, snatched the dishtowel from Aldo.

"Since when do you have good taste in women?" Aldo mumbled, taking up a position on the dark side.

Too intent on studying the board, I didn't reply. When Ilse finished the dishes she joined us in the living room. Every so often she sipped her wine. The pieces were being whittled down. After an hour, I took a bathroom break, at which time Ilse removed a bunch of letters from her handbag and began addressing them.

"Can I say that I think you're good for him?"

"You already did."

Aldo finished his wine, poured some more into Ilse's glass and refilled his own. He drank. "I've never seen him so content. You know what I mean?" Aldo said, allowing the wine to loosen his tongue.

"It sounds as if his life wasn't going so well."

Aldo moved closer, said almost in a whisper, "There have been nights I'd have to go out and look for him."

"In this city?"

"He has his favorite haunts. Fortunately, I know most of them," Aldo said, drinking more wine. "What are you writing, if you don't mind me asking?"

"Thank you notes to viewers for saying nice things about Mr. Charlton."

"It must be sweet working for a class act like him."

"I'll relay your message."

Aldo peered at what Ilse was writing. "Anyone ever tell you about your hand-writing?"

"I know it's sloppy." Aldo kept looking. "Are you a handwriting analyst?"

"You're pretty sharp. After I broke up with Cindy, she's my ex, I didn't want to go back to being a chemist so I learned something else for fun."

"What do you see?" Ilse asked, as I came in and sat down. "David, Aldo was about to analyze my handwriting."

"I didn't know you did that?"

"I thought I told you." I shook my head. "I'm in a fog half the time."

"What about the other half?" Ilse asked.

Aldo grinned. "You guys have the same sense of humor. That's important. Cindy never laughed at anything I said. She only laughed at what I did."

"I should be on my way," Ilse said, "let you finish your game."

"Stay," Aldo said, adding "I'll button my lip."

"It isn't that, Aldo. I've an early day tomorrow."

As Ilse got to her feet, several letters fell from her lap. I stooped down to pick them up. The paper had the same feel as the envelope of the letter Ilse received from Argentina and the letters I got from Uncle Kurt. It might be a good idea, I thought, to ask Aldo to analyze Uncle Kurt's handwriting when he sobered up.

Aldo was losing power when I moved my queen to d6 and said checkmate, settling the game in one swift stroke. "You foxed me, 'Willy the Kid'..."

As I was putting the chess pieces to bed, I felt Ilse's eyes on me. "I'm going," she whispered, "Ky's got some people coming in early he wants me to meet and greet. Okay, 'Big Cat'?"

"Whatever you say? Are we on for tomorrow night?"

"I'll call you."

"Is anything wrong?"

"What could be wrong?" she said, her eyes beginning to tear.

"Let me get you a cab."

"Don't bother."

"I want to talk to you."

She put her finger to her lips, then to mine. "We'll talk. You'll tell me you love me. After that, who knows?"

Once Ilse was gone, Aldo woke up—groggy, but talkative. "Where's Ilse?"

"She went home."

"You're not angry?"

"No, Aldo, I'm not angry."

"Did I ever tell you you're a pretty nice guy?" Aldo said, throwing his arms around me.

I took the brunt of Aldo's cheese-like chest, watched him negotiate the distance across the hall. Once I was alone, I opened the cabinet above the sink, found a glass and went into my office. I removed a bottle of whiskey from an unlocked drawer of my desk, filled the glass halfway and finished it.

I'd been careless. Revealing things to Ilse was a calculated risk. Telling Aldo about my past was simply an attempt to relate to someone I was fond of and had grown to trust as a friend. Ilse's reaction to the 'Willy the Kid' remark was plain to see. She made no attempt to hide it.

The bottle was three-quarters empty when I called Ilse. I thought, all she could do was to tell me I was a pretty good fuck for a guy my age and blow me off."

"What do you want?" she said, before I could say hello.

"I never showed you my work."

"You wake me up to tell me that?"

"You weren't sleeping."

"What was I doing?"

"What you usually do when your lover isn't around."

"You have a filthy mind." I laughed. "What's your real name?"

"I told you."

"Tell me again. Tell me a story I can wrap my arms around."

Even half-drunk, I knew what she was doing. She was masturbating to my words. She was using whatever I said to get her off. "Yes, I'll tell you," I said. "Carl knows my real name. So does his father. They know many things about many people. The methods of torture they use are quite effective. Squeezing the blood out of human arms a drop at a time, ripping the tongues out of human brains, burning what's left so there's no proof and in the bargain fertilizing the fields."

I heard her panting at the other end; soon I was touching myself too, doing what little boys did in dark places in schools, attics, basements and bathrooms in winter with the smell of steam and paint, when the hurting needed to come out if only to relieve itself a little, the pain that once released shot a kind of salty-sweet painkiller. Afterwards, bothered by thoughts of what would happen if I got caught by the priest or one of the sisters or by someone who ratted me out to get special favors.

There was silence at both ends. Finally, I said, "My father was a member of the Nazi party."

"Didn't you say you were nine when you left Germany?"

"I was old enough to remember stories my mother told me."

'Was your mother a Nazi too?"

"Go to sleep, Ilse."

"I can't sleep."

"Even now?"

"Yes, only If you were lying next to me I would be sleepy."

"What's the use?"

"I haven't told Carl anything. And, I won't if you promise not to ask me to help you steal a painting from my sister."

"Ilse, I only want to have a look."

"Can't you see anything from behind the blindness of your self-sacrifice?"

"Until my Uncle Kurt wrote and told me what was going on in Germany in 1923 and later, until he gave me specifics about my mother, I was losing interest."

"Listen to me, David, we can walk away from this and keep walking."

"With Carl and his contacts always looking for us? No thank you."

"I wish I had an Uncle Kurt."

"Why is that?"

"I'd like to be as dedicated as you in finding out why my mother never writes or visits or asks when Trudi and I will visit."

"Then, help me. Perhaps, we can find out about your mother in the process."

"Like killing two birds with one stone?"

"It's possible."

"No, it isn't possible. You don't realize what you're up against."

"I'd rather fight them head-on than wait. Ilse, if I do nothing, do you think Carl and those reborn-Nazis with him will let me live knowing what I know?"

"What are you saying?"

"I'm as good as dead—unless I get lucky."

"You're frightening me, David."

"Am I?"

IX. MARTY SUNSHINE

imon Wiesenthal was a man people called, "the conscience of the Holocaust." He'd been after Nazi war criminals since the end of the Second World War. In 1965, I wrote to Mr. Wiesenthal at the Jewish Documents Center in Vienna and asked for information concerning the whereabouts of members of the Mannheim family in Berlin—Ernst or Freda. I said Freda was Jewish and asked about Anton Kessler as well.

I received a letter back stating that the Center didn't look for missing persons, only missing criminals. They suggested I try the American Red Cross or German authorities, though it was Mr. Wiesenthal's feeling, based on his experience, that too many years had gone by. He personally offered his deepest sympathy for my missing family, said he too lost members of his own family. (Eighty-nine to be exact) "As for Anton Kessler," he wrote, "he died in Auschwitz in 1943."

I went for a walk to clear my head, felt ghosts in the air around me and wasn't sure what to do. They didn't touch me, yet I felt touched. They didn't overtake me yet I felt their presence, a covey of souls not quite real. I slowed my gait hoping they'd come down from their perch. All they did was slow the speed of their airborne perambulation to a ghostly glide. I sensed they wanted to tell me something, but I heard no voice call or even whisper.

Then I heard the sound of a band, people marching in a parade; men and women roused by songs being played in a rising crescendo. Spooked by the ear-piercing brass, the thump of drums, the ghosts vanished. Once the sounds abated the ghosts reappeared, tagged along, their frayed wings flying beside my threadbare dream. One of them even followed me into the building where I lived, into my apartment after I closed the door in their face.

This ghost reminded me of someone I hadn't seen for a long time. She didn't look like a ghost—dressed in clothes that were out of fashion. A felt hat with a silly-looking feather sat precariously atop her head; a white sweater with pearl buttons, several unbuttoned and no bra. A beaded bag swung from her arm as she moved about, her derriere doing most of the moving inside a tight-fitting black wool skirt. She took a cigarette from a gold case in her pocketbook and lighted it.

I wanted to squeeze the smoke out of the lungs beneath her unrestricted breasts. I kept my distance until I could make up my mind as to the reliability of someone who presumably had crossed the barrier between the living world we knew and the world no one could see. I checked her face, the longish nose, the soft full lips, the blue-gray eyes and upswept bobby-pinned brown hair.

"I'm your mother," she said, "Don't you recognize me?"

"How can you be my mother? I'm older than you."

"If I lived I'd be almost a hundred years old."

"Then, you're not real." She didn't answer.

"Do you ever think about me?" she asked. I nodded. "Do you ever see me?"

"I see you when I'm alone…in my mind."

"Isn't what you see in your mind as real to you as seeing someone on the street?"

"Not quite, but you make a good point. Sometimes you wake me up in the morning."

"Do I scream?"

"So loud I have to hold my ears."

"Do you have any idea what was done to me?"

"I watched you die."

"You remember?"

"Of course, I remember."

"You're a good boy." She said the words as though I was still a child.

"I've spent my entire life looking for the ones responsible."

"God knows it was my dying wish."

"I've done my best."

"You were a brave boy, Willy."

"Don't call me that. My name is David."

"David's a nice name. Your great-grandfather's name was David. He was a religious man. He put on phylactery."

"What's phylactery?"

"It's part of a religious ritual. On weekday mornings you bind your left arm with a leather strap and pray.

"Pray for what?"

"That you don't cut off the circulation."

"That isn't funny. I told them where you were."

"They tricked you."

"Tell me, will I ever be released from my promise?"

"I can't tell you what to do. Only your conscience can." I found a glass and filled it with whiskey. "You drink too much, Willy."

"I told you my name is David. How do you know how much I drink?"

"I hear it in your voice. Perhaps, you'll be rewarded for your efforts."

"Why did they torture you? What did they want?"

"What do men always want?"

"Who was it?"

"I can't."

"Why not?"

"I shouldn't have come."

"At least tell me which one of Kessler's paintings contains the clue?"

"You'll know it when you see it." I stared at this woman in disbelief. "If I told you it wouldn't be fair."

"What do you mean, 'fair?' Were those brutes fair? Did they play by the rules?"

"When you were a boy you wanted to grow up like them. I saw it in your eyes. You were entranced by men without scruples, without a shred of human decency."

"I've grown up."

"I was afraid you were becoming mesmerized by the way they marched, the way they looked in their uniforms."

"They were strong and seemed so sure of themselves. Can't you tell me anything that might help? Or would you rather I die without finding out?"

"Sometimes you have to do things you don't like, to survive."

"Like what?"

"Whatever it takes."

"Give me an example?"

"You're not a teacher. I'm not your student."

"What are you?"

"What do I look like?"

I took another look at this woman who seemed to be my

mother and said, "You look like a prostitute."

"Whatever it takes, Willy." I heard her call my name only it sounded like a scream I'd heard all my life, "Willie-e-e-e!" I covered my ears.

"What do you know about my father?"

"Don't you remember what I told you?"

"I was nine. I need to know more."

"He thought every man wanted a piece of me. I told him he captured my heart from the first time I saw him."

"Is that why he played chess—to capture the Queen?"

"He was confused about what to believe in, who to believe in."

"Tell me what do you believe in?" There was no answer. "If I have to spend the rest of my life doing this, could you at least stop screaming?"

There was a knock at the door. "Did you sleep with Kessler?" I asked, turning toward the door. It was Aldo. I let him in. When I turned back she was gone. I told him what happened. Aldo said his mother was alive and never talked to him. The phone rang. I motioned to Aldo with my head to become scarce, a signal he understood. Once Aldo was gone, I got on. The person's voice was sharp, jumpy. "It's Marty, can we meet someplace?"

"Marty—what's it about?"

"How would you like to do a sequel to my first book?"

"You're joking."

"I'm quite serious."

"Sounds okay. When would be a convenient time?"

"What about this evening?"

"It's half-past ten. I'm about to go to bed."

"Oh yes, Charlton's assistant."

"Her name is Ilse van Ness."

"Pretty name."

"What about lunch tomorrow? There's a little bar on the west side between Forty-Fifth and...?"

"I know the place," Marty broke in, "Shall we say one o'clock?"

"That works."

Once I was off the phone I had the strangest feeling Sunshine, who had suffered more than the average person, was fearful. It kept me up most of the night. By the time I fell asleep it was close to the hour I was supposed to meet Marty. Realizing I was late, I dressed and dashed out the door.

The bar on 45th Street was crowded. There were people everywhere, with conversations going on simultaneously, traveling in all directions; sounds of clinking glasses, china, silverware, shuffling feet and legs of wooden chairs scraping along the sawdust floor.

The maître d showed me to a small table midway between the bar and the kitchen along the east wall. The location of the small round table provided a familiar position, offering a good view in all directions. A waiter in black trousers, white shirt, black bowtie, came by. I ordered a mug of draught beer.

At one-ten, I lowered my eyes to check my watch. When I looked up, Marty was pushing his way towards the table.

"Sorry I'm late," he said, looking like he'd had a better night's sleep than I.

I was surprised at the easy manner of the man who sounded so edgy on the phone the night before. "Have you ordered?"

I shook my head. The waiter appeared. "What can I get for you gentlemen?" he asked, his pen poised.

"Steak sandwich and a refill," I said, tapping my empty mug while Marty scanned the menu.

"And, you, sir?"

"I'll have the same with a green salad." I wondered, does a man order a green salad at a time when his life is in danger?

"Be right out," the waiter said, quickly on his way.

"Mind if I ask a question?"

"Fire away."

"What was so urgent?"

"Not a thing—at least not anymore."

"I'm glad to hear it."

"If we'd have met yesterday who knows what might have happened?"

"I'm not sure what you mean."

"Do you remember the book you did for me?"

"Of course. Were you really pleased?"

"Very pleased."

The waiter arrived with our drinks. "The book made my father and mother happy, but also sad. To be drawn back into the early days of their marriage when they were still young and in their own country. It can be filled with mixed emotions."

"Is there to be a new book?"

"It's possible at some future date."

"What was it you wanted me to do?"

"After my father died I found myself going through his things. There was a black book among his belongings. In it he talks about the work he did during the war."

"What kind of work?"

"In one of the camps."

"The death camps?"

The waiter brought our lunch, placed each order in front of each of us. "Will there be anything else?"

"Not at the moment," Marty said.

"Was it where Holbein painted peaches?"

"Were you a history major?"

"Where?" I asked, pressing my fingers around my steak sandwich.

"Dachau."

I took a bite, feeling the blood trickle through spaces in my teeth. When I finished chewing, I said, "Germany is a hobby of mine."

"I was hoping to use one of my father's contacts at the embassy. It didn't work out."

"How was your father able to avoid arrest?"

"The Nuremberg Trials were a farce. It gave the world its pound of flesh. A long list of swine got away, my father included." It was Sunshine's turn to squeeze his fingers around his steak sandwich and take a bite.

"I don't understand. You spoke so highly of him."

"He was my inspiration. He put in forty-five years as a salesman."

"What did he sell?"

"America."

"Come on, Marty."

"What's the difference? The reason for my wanting to see you has been made superfluous. Let's just say I found an avid reader."

"I thought you said your father's friends at the embassy were of no help."

"True enough," Marty said, as he finished his beer. "Nevertheless a friend emerged. Hopefully, there will be others."

The magnitude of Marty's disclosure showed in his florid puffed-out cheeks. He got to his feet, put down more than enough to pay for lunch, stuck out his hand and said: "It's been a pleasure, David. Perhaps, we can do it again sometime."

On my way home, I tried to make sense of things like gaps in time; years I spent floundering. Uncle Kurt's letters spoke a different language. How could he have been in a position to hear, see, and smell what was going on; to know so much about the Nazi butchers and still be alive?

X. Circle of Engagement

lose to the dinner hour, Aldo barged in without knocking. I swung my desk chair around, pulled my revolver from its holster and pointed it at the intruder.

"What's with the Bogart routine?"

"Practice makes perfect. Besides, don't you know how to knock?"

"How about if I have someone announce my imminent arrival?"

"Anyone ever tell you your sense of humor might get you into trouble someday?"

"Never mind that. Did you see the six o'clock news? Someone knocked off Kyle Charlton." I stuffed the gun inside my belt. "Careful you don't shoot off your dick."

I went into the living room, snapped on the TV. The well-groomed newscaster looked dead serious. "Kyle Charlton was found in his suite at the Olympia Towers by the maid. He'd been shot once in the temple, making it appear the work of a professional. Police believe the victim was murdered sometime during the night. Police Chief Braden has assumed personal charge of the investigation. He feels the coroner's report will confirm the case as a homicide, admitting he has no leads thus far as to who might have committed the crime. He advises anyone with information to call the local precinct. Mayor Janiro has already proclaimed this coming Tuesday as a day of mourning by ordering flags in the city to be flown at half-mast."

I snapped off the TV. "I have to find Ilse," I said, getting to my feet.

"I just saw her."

"Where?"

"She was being interviewed by some broad as she was getting into a taxi."

I got my cell phone, punched in Ilse's number.

"Have you heard the news?" she asked.

"Yeah. Are you okay?"

"I'm still in shock."

"Where are you?"

"I'm on my way over to the Towers. The police think I may have been the last person to see Ky alive."

"When was that?"

"After I spoke to you." Her voice sounded shaky.

I felt sick to my stomach. "Ilse, why?"

"It wasn't like that. He needed someone to talk to."

"What did he say?"

"Ky belonged to a select fraternity, people who only tell you what they want you to know. And, they don't make unnecessary enemies. He was admired and trusted because his guests knew they'd be presented in the best possible light, despite occasional lapses like with your friend Sunshine."

I let Ilse's remark slide. "Do you have any idea who might want Ky out of the fraternity?"

"Last night, when I got there the lights were turned off. Ky was sitting behind his desk, his voice barely audible. He was calmer than I'd ever seen him. It gave me the creeps. He said something about finally having the guts to risk his own neck. He said he was tired of pretending. He admitted that some of his guests got under his skin because they did things he could only talk about."

"Wasn't that his job?"

"It sounded to me as though he wanted to act on his own convictions."

"Any particular one?"

"Most likely the one that got him killed."

"That's too bad."

"Yes, it is. David. What do you know about Marty Sunshine?"

"Not much. He called last night, asked if I could meet him someplace. I told him I was about to go to bed."

"And?"

"I had lunch with him today. He seemed relieved, said the matter was in good hands."

"Did he happen to say in 'whose good hands'?"

"A friend's."

"Ky spent most of his life speaking as if he'd been educated at Cambridge and wondering if his time would ever come."

"Time for what?"

"He felt outside the circle of engagement. I think he was ticked off the other night because Marty Sunshine tasted life in ways Ky could only dream about."

"I wouldn't call what Marty Sunshine went through tasting life. He endured the worst kinds of torture. "

"You talk as if you know a lot about it?"

"Ilse, my love…" I said, stopping, not wanting to say something I might regret.

"What?" Ilse asked, displeased with my reluctance to go further.

"Call me when you're through."

"Wait. Can you get in touch with Mr. Sunshine?"

"I'll see what I can do."

I retrieved Marty's number from my voice mail, called the number—no luck. Going through my files, I realized I didn't keep records as far back as the Sixties. Then, I remembered Marty's foundation, *One World*.

A Miss Gehringer answered the phone. She informed me that Mr. Sunshine was away on business, and that he left no forwarding address or number where he could be reached. She had the impersonal tone of a private secretary down so pat I was impressed, even as I tried to make the woman understand the importance of my call. I finally gave up convinced she had strict orders not to divulge anything regarding Marty's whereabouts.

The police questioned Ilse about her untimely visit to Kyle Charlton's apartment. When they were satisfied she was telling them the truth, they allowed her to go, with a reminder not to leave town without first notifying them. As soon as she was on the street, she called me. I told her I had nothing for her on Sunshine. There was a momentary hesitation before Ilse said: "Get a good night's sleep, David. I'll call you tomorrow. Bye."

Following Ilse's curt farewell, I decided to get something to eat. The food wasn't very good. Outside the restaurant, the cold dug into my chest like a sharp tool a convict might use to tunnel out of prison. I turned up the collar of my jacket, walked the rest of the way home. Something was wrong. I'd been trying to lay off the hard stuff. How many times had I given in lately? Last night? Last week? It was hard remembering as I slammed into my apartment.

I didn't turn on the lights. Instead, I went directly to the liquor cabinet, stuck my hand inside, pulled out a half-full bottle of whiskey. One shot should do the trick. Not good enough. I had another to straighten out the curveball I felt spinning my way...

to get a piece of the ball the way good hitters did even when they were fooled by the pitch.

It was four A.M. when I woke up half-undressed and spread out on the couch like a Sunday comic strip. The whiskey bottle was on its side, some of its contents spilled on the rug. Shaky underpinnings told me I'd spilled more into me. I steadied myself, made my way into the bedroom; sprawled on the bed and fell fast to sleep.

Next morning, the face in the vanity mirror told me what the years brought; a marked up scorecard with many erasures. I showered, awakened the little nerve endings I knew would send me back into the game no matter what the score.

Ilse called. "What time is it?"

"Eleven. I tried you earlier."

"I was in the shower."

"Can you be ready in an hour?"

"What's up?"

"Be outside. I'll tell you when I get there."

Before I could answer, she cut the connection. I put on a fresh shirt, shoulder holster, then jacket. I was getting used to it, the way men with a hernia get used to wearing a truss. As I was leaving, the phone rang. It was Marty. He asked if I'd heard about Kyle Charlton. I said I heard it on the news. Marty said Charlton was on a mission to contact someone in Germany.

"What's his name?"

"I don't know his name. I contact him through a PO Box in Berlin."

"Was the contact made?"

"No."

"How can you be sure?"

"Charlton was tortured. There are places on the human

anatomy if touched a certain way that can produce excruciating pain. Not even forensic experts can detect where the pressure is applied. Kyle Charlton was shot once in the left temple to make it appear as if it was a professional hit. Open and shut. Technically the bullet killed him."

"Tell the police."

"And, then, what? It's possible the people who killed Charlton were convinced he was telling them the truth, that I didn't pass on to him what they want."

"What do they want?"

"It's a long story, David."

"What you're really saying is you don't trust me."

"I didn't have to call. Besides, you have enough on your plate."

"Do you mean Ilse?"

"Is that her name?"

Seeing the time, I locked the door of my apartment. Walking down the stairs, I continued our conversation. "What if you're wrong, won't they come after you?" Marty didn't answer. "For God-sakes Marty, go to the police."

"It won't do any good. If Charlton didn't spill the beans he may have put the evidence in what he felt was a safe place."

"They found him at home. Nothing was touched."

"You miss their ability to see every inch of his apartment without disturbing a hair."

"I know about that. They paid me a visit too, to fix the furnace."

"What do you know about that?"

"Come on, Marty, isn't there something I can do for you?"

"Watch what you say and to whom," Sunshine said, more openly. "These people are growing steadily in power and number."

"What people?"

"The world is always on the lookout for a magician to pull a rabbit out of a hat. There's something you should know, David."

"I don't have much time. Ilse is picking me up in a few minutes."

"My first book told about what goes on in the military, how people are thrown away for the sake of a system that blunders in the name of humanity. Human beings don't work in the State Department. To get the key to the washroom you have to surrender your integrity and present yourself to the world as a patriot for a government that considers you expendable. Everyone's expendable in this system. Examine it. Never mind the money. It's printed for the masses to play with. Top shelf is where to look. You might see who holds the reins, twirls the power 'round their little finger and says when, where and how the next carnage goes down."

I'd reached the street. My eyes searched in both directions. "Here's the best part," Sunshine said. "One day I get a call from the owner of the furnace company. We meet for drinks, talk. He tries to convince me he isn't interested in Herr Hitler anymore. He said he liked the idea of *One World* even before I wrote the book."

"What made them stop trusting you?"

"Who knows why things happen? Perhaps, I got careless."

"You wanted me to be your messenger. My father was killed in that line of work."

"My father escaped. Did it ever occur to you that we follow a predetermined path begun by our fathers—whether we like it or not?"

"What do they know about me?" I asked, skipping the philosophy lesson.

"You're a little fish, Menard, but you've piqued their curiosity."

"What about Ilse?"

"She does what's she's told."

"Why? What is she afraid of?"

"Perhaps, she knows what's good for her," Marty said, adding, "Don't think I see the world in its grotesque aspects because I'm bitter. Blood stains the parchment of every Bible and history book. When it's quiet listen to the sound the dead make beneath the earth. I hear them sometimes. If you listen hard you might be able to hear them too."

I could feel Sunshine's pain. It was palpable, a growing madness. "One last question, Marty?"

"Shoot."

"If I happen to get lucky where do I deliver the merchandise?"

"PO Box 015, Kurfürstendamm, Berlin."

"Are you sure?"

"Of course I'm sure."

"If I give you my e-mail address can you get it to this party?"

"I'll try."

"Tell him I need to hear from him soon."

"Are we talking about the same person?"

"I don't know, Marty. And, if I did you'd be better off not knowing."

"For someone with no previous experience you catch on quick."

"Thanks. What about yourself?"

"There may be a way out for me yet. Remember, I'm a survivor."

"Good luck."

"Save the good luck wishes for yourself. You'll need it. *Auf wiedersehen.*"

XI. DACHAU

Ilse pulled to the curb, turned my way and said, "You clean up nice." I took the compliment in stride, slid into the passenger seat of the yellow sports car. Ilse looked stunning in a blue silk dress. It was the kind of silk that clung to her in all the right places, made me jealous of silkworms. "Sorry I'm late," she said, "As I was leaving I got a call from Captain Braden."

"You didn't steal this beauty, did you?"

"It was Ky's."

The car yanked away from the curb. I said, "Go easy on the turns."

"What's the matter, James, didn't you get a good night's sleep?"

"I slept like a log," I lied.

"I didn't. It was cold in bed without you."

"What if the police spot you driving Ky's car?"

"I'll take my chances."

"What do you have in mind?"

Ilse turned on 72nd Street, pointed the chrome grille of the classic MG toward the West Side Highway. Getting no answer, I asked: "Why all the mystery?"

"Doesn't everyone like a good mystery?"

I snugged on a Yankee baseball cap. Once over the GW, Ilse moved the car into the left lane, pressed down on the gas pedal. The car surged ahead.

"I love suburbia, don't you—the smell of burnt rubber."

She looked at me, said with sudden passion. "I love you."

"Do you?" She nodded, smiling. I ran the palm of my hand along Ilse's thigh.

I closed my eyes, thought of Marty Sunshine and 015 Kurfürstendamm; of Uncle Kurt and what happened at that address.

By the time we reached the Jersey shore the air cloyed. Grass grew in clumps, wild and woody. The ocean salt mixed with the dross of industry, bolstered by a nation's mindset that felt free to practice chemistry in the open air. Kyle Charlton's beach house was set a distance away from the other houses.

Ilse parked the car; we got out and walked. Ilse reached into her handbag. My hand slid inside my jacket. "You won't need that," she said, taking out a key.

The shades were drawn, our welcome the clammy feeling of mildew and dust. Ilse snapped on a light. The furniture in the room was new. It smelled of cheap lacquer. Behind a tier of interconnecting modules, high in the mountainous wall-regions of the square-shaped room, row upon row of books sat on cliff dweller shelves.

The books weren't stacked in alphabetical order, but by category: Humor, Mystery, History, Adventure, Spiritual, among others. The floor was tiled in some geometric pattern; area rugs lay under two leather chairs like sleeping dogs, while a stone fireplace stood in the center of the room—a stack of birch logs and brass implements close by. Lights were recessed in the ceiling and regulated from a panel of wall switches. The cold atmosphere didn't quite suggest curling up with a good book, even with a fire. And all the time I heard the gulls, their mocking laughter at the futility of landlocked humans.

While Ilse checked the rest of the house, I focused my attention on the bound volumes. Drawing closer, I sniffed the aroma of cigars, noticed a box of Cuban-made *Monte Cristo's,* and that one of the leather chairs had an indent in its cushion.

Ilse's shoes made so much noise they sounded Dutch. I turned and called, "The bags under his eyes were well-earned."

"Ky liked to give that impression," Ilse said, as she returned. "One of my duties was to read a book, tell him what it was about and brief him on the juicier parts."

"That isn't what he said."

"He skimmed pages, had acting lessons, a make-up artist...a professional lighting consultant."

"He fooled me."

"Good actors often do. Still, there was a different person sitting behind Ky's desk the night I went to see him."

"Are you saying it's never too late to learn to read?"

"I'm saying a man like you, being familiar with books, might find the one book that made Ky believe he could do something useful for mankind."

I followed Ilse into the kitchen. "Was he that much of an idealist?"

"Ky's style was to press for the inside story. If his guest was a prick he'd hammer him. Mostly he played the role of genial host, using his boyish eagerness to stimulate his guests into revealing something beyond what was between the covers of the book they'd written. That style made him rich and famous."

Ilse had opened the windows and raised the shades, White curtains hung loose and free, blowing ever so slightly. The appliances were stainless, with cherry cabinetry, black granite countertops and no food in the fridge. The closets, cabinets and drawers turned up nothing more than brooms, brushes, cooking utensils, silverware and pots and pans as shiny as the day they were bought. An expensive CD player hid out in one of the cabinets, with four concealed speakers surrounding the room like watchdogs.

"He liked coming here."

"It has all the warmth of a German pillbox."

"How would you know?"

I let Ilse's remark slide. "I'll check out the stacks."

I was about to climb the ladder when once again I felt her eyes. I glanced over my shoulder like someone who'd played the 'looking game,' she with the eyes of a woman who'd looked all her life for the man she could put on a pedestal next to the portrait of her father.

"You were quiet on the ride out."

"I didn't want to spoil your serenity."

"Did Marty Sunshine ever get in touch?"

"As a matter of fact he did."

"And?"

"He may not have long to live."

"Then, he's responsible."

"You said yourself Ky wanted action. Well, he got what he wanted."

"That's a bit rough, isn't it?"

I took her hand and kissed it, took a soft bite from the meaty underside.

"Is my 'Big Cat' hungry?"

"We better stick to business."

"The books seem too obvious to hide something, don't you think? There must be over a thousand."

"Twenty-two hundred and fifty, give or take a few."

"How can you tell?"

"I count with my eyes."

"Can you find Mr. Sunshine's book?"

"What about in the contemporary-spiritual stack?"

I climbed the ladder, scanned the rows. My fingers lightly touched the spine of each book. Two rows down I found a copy of *One World,* took the hardcover book in my hands, opened it and flipped through the pages. I ran my fingers along both sides of the front and back covers for any irregularity. Figuring I'd done my best, I was coming down the ladder when I remembered something Marty said. He used the expression, "top shelf." It sent me back up to the top. No rarefied air here and I'd no reason to suspect I'd find anything. But, as I ran my hand across a row of books I came across a thin black volume without a jacket. I pulled it, started down. "I'd like to have a better look," I said, trying to make it seem the book was a shot in the dark rather than a valuable find.

"May I see?" Ilse asked, extending her hand, as I came down the ladder. She flipped through the pages of *One World* without saying a word. Seeing the other book was worn, making its title hard to read, she gave both books back to me—again, no words. By the time we left, everything was the way we'd found it. She locked up and we were on our way.

The police would investigate. They'd find out Ky had a beach house and investigate further. They'd find fingerprints. They might even give Ilse a hard time for not mentioning the place to them. She'd say she didn't think it was important—that Mr. Charlton seldom went there.

On the ride back to the city, I saw the strain on Ilse's face. She pretended to be perfectly capable of taking the news of Kyle

Charlton's death in stride. Her false front started to fade at about the same time as her makeup. I made small talk. Ilse responded, grateful it appeared to have her mind distracted by a conversation of little import—if only for the moment.

Crossing over the George Washington, Ilse turned to me and said, "Want some company?"

"You're tired. Go home and rest."

"I want to be with you," she said, as we reached my place.

I leaned over to kiss her. Our lips met, soft and sweet. "I'll call if I find out anything important," I said, getting out.

Ilse leaned towards me. "David, tell me to cook for you. Tell me to make love to you. Tell me you want to marry me and take care of me. Tell me something."

I stood dumbly at the curb waiting for words to come to me. I didn't want to press her about her part in helping me get into Carl's apartment. Finally, I said, "I trust you with my life."

"I'm not sure I trust you with mine," she said, driving off.

Later, after a couple of drinks, I sat at my desk. *One World,* Marty Sunshine's faux crack at fascism, glistened in its shiny jacket. I was tempted to read a few pages, but realizing time was a problem I picked up the other book instead. I turned it on its side as if it were a flatulent baby, pushed my index finger inside the binding until it split. Flattened against the spine was a thin packet wrapped in tissue paper. Inside was a roll of 35mm film with words written on a label that read: Dachau, 1942–1944. There was also a handwritten note in German. I translated as best I could. "In the summer of 1943, *Kommandant* Kraus asked me to photograph activities at the camp. Naturally, I was careful to show the Jews holding new blankets, lying on clean mattresses, eating decent food. We used the most recent arrivals. I don't remember how many rolls of film I provided Kraus with, but there were many. One I kept, careful not to develop the film in Germany.

"I took the photographs the day the furnaces were upgraded to double capacity. A small ceremony was held at the site. A bottle of champagne I personally selected christened the new furnace. Besides a few generals, there was *Kommandant* Kraus and Bruno Schneider, a man known only to the Fuehrer and those men directly responsible to him. It was an honor for me to stand alongside the man they called 'The Furnace-maker.'

"We drank a glass of champagne, then another. The furnace was hot. Bruno Schneider was sweating. He summoned one of the Jews given the privilege of cleaning up after the bodies were burned to sweep up the glass from the broken bottle of champagne. Herr Schneider turned his back for an instant. The half-crazed Jew shoved him into the furnace door. Herr Schneider was scalded. He screamed the sound Jews made once they entered the showers and realized they'd been locked in and saw the vapor coming down on them like the wrath of God, choking off their air supply until they clawed and scratched one another in a mad stampede to get out. The Jew was thrown into the oven by two of our men, the door left slightly ajar so we could hear his screams. Herr Schneider was badly burned over his arms and one side of his face. He was placed on a stretcher and taken to the infirmary. As he was being carried out, I got several good shots with my Leica."

The note was signed: L. Brennermann.

XII. My Gestapo Friends

I couldn't sleep. I got out of bed, unlocked the drawer of my desk, took out the letters and began to read, They send me to Munich. Some say my strategy on the chessboard paves the way for battles won by our Panzers in Russia and North Africa.

In the autumn of 1943 I live in a small apartment on the Odeonsplatz. Among the artists and sculptors the illusion of freedom manifests itself, carefully maintained for all to see. I live comfortably, but as I suspect, I'm being watched. Never out of the sight of those seedy looking men in drab suits and rumpled raincoats who sit in mud-caked automobiles drinking cold coffee, smoking cigarettes, waiting for me to do something to send them into action so they can take advantage of their expert training. Meanwhile, they file daily reports as to my behavior. It seems to me the Gestapo exist for the sole purpose of finding a mote of dust to crush with their boot.

I blame no one but myself and accept this way of life without a peep. If they gush with pride as they tell me how much I've helped the cause, I act pleased without letting it affect my outward behavior. Perhaps, I'm as pleased as they think. Still, I must be careful not to say anything that might be misconstrued. Nothing I say or do must give them a reason to suspect I do this work not out of great admiration for our leader, but because I love my country, my family and my friends—the few that are left.

Closing my eyes at night I see what I won't allow myself to see with my eyes open. It's in darkness my own thoughts are illuminated. The spring of 1944 brings greater concern about the war. Russia, thought to be dead and buried in the snow, raises to her knees, then to her feet. By early spring, she's on the offensive. There are rumors that England and the United States are preparing to invade. Field Marshall Erwin Rommel, our most respected general, is called upon by the Fuehrer to advise Generals Keitel, Jodl and Von Rundstedt on how to shore up coastline defenses in France.

They match me against a man I can only describe as a scarecrow inside a filthy suit. Yellow skinned, nearly bald, with hollow eyes, he wears gold spectacles without glass. I find it uncomfortable playing against him since I can feel his beady eyes press heavily on me. I take less time deciding my next move. It costs me. I do something silly. He apologizes as he takes a valuable piece. Rather than continue, I ask for a bathroom break.

With my concentration broken, I find myself noticing things I'd overlooked. For one thing, the window in the lavatory has bars on the outside and is nailed shut from the inside. I hear a sound and turn, soon to be joined at the urinals by my opponent. The Gestapo man follows him inside, but is called away. I try not to pay attention to the man who stands next to me.

"You don't look like one of them," he says, in a low voice. I don't answer. "Are you?" I say nothing. "The *Kommandant's* adjutant and I play chess sometimes. He got me a reprieve."

"I don't understand," I reply obtusely. "Are you a prisoner of war?"

"I'm a Jew. See!"

He rolls up his sleeve. His arm has a number tattooed on it. "Where are you from?"

"I used to live in Potsdam. I now reside in Dachau."

"The camp?"

"Not a camp for boys and girls." He laughs until he begins to cough. "Excuse me. I must be coming down with something."

"Don't they feed you?"

"They don't feed. They don't treat. They butcher. First a charade, then the promise work will set us free. We're dead on our feet, lousy with bugs and disease. They tell us to clean up in the showers. No one returns from the showers, but if one refuses to go they shoot you. They play Strauss waltzes, using something other than soap and water. It's called Zyklon B. You know about that?" I shake my head. "Crystallized prussic acid... It gets inside and stops the screaming. The bodies lie in piles until the SS and forced labor remove them, extract gold from teeth, cut off hair so when they shovel the bodies into the crematoria the smell doesn't offend people who live nearby. I'd like to examine the noses of the people living in Dachau, how it is they don't smell burning flesh. The furnaces run day and night. The man who built the furnaces, I don't know his name other than what I hear people call him." He bends towards me and whispers: "The Furnace-maker. He's the inventor, an expert in the field. They're all experts at making people disappear."

"How do you know so much?"

"I told you."

I stand incredulous, not sure if the man is deranged or telling the truth. One look at him suggests both possibilities. He sees the look on my face and says, "Don't you believe me?"

"How can that be?"

"Pay us a visit sometime. Who knows how long I'll be there. But, new guests arrive every day."

"I'd like to see..." I begin, when the Gestapo man opens the door. "Come on, come on. You're taking too long."

The man and I return to the chessboard. He's less nervous when we resume and finish our game. That night in bed I can't get the image of the man's face out of my mind. Perhaps, I think in some small way I've restored his will to go on.

I give the matter no further thought until I'm told the man I report to every day has been replaced by a new man for having mistakenly sent a truckload of Jews to Dachau instead of to Auschwitz. The night before he's to leave for the eastern front he asks me to join him for a drink in a local beer hall. He thinks his star is on the rise. He's out of his mind. But, he's buying cognac and talking to every woman who looks our way. He says he's been told on several occasions to offer me favors within reason and to keep a tight surveillance on my movements. "They don't want to lose their number one pigeon," he says, laughing.

The new man in charge, fat, with oily skin and head shaven clean, is a pencil-pusher from Hamburg who worked in an umbrella factory before the war. His hands are covered with newsprint from poring over daily reports. He has two secretaries and a stenographer but insists upon carefully going over their work. He doesn't say much, but I can tell he's interested in chess. I feel him peering over my shoulder on several occasions. One day, he decides to try his luck with me. I tell him I'd rather play for the party than for pleasure. He insists that I do him this one small favor. We play and I contrive to have the match end in a draw; a great victory for the pencil pusher from Hamburg.

A week later I receive a letter from the camp thanking me for playing one last game with Nathan Brodsky. It says, If the name doesn't ring a bell, I will tell you that he was European chess champion from 1930–1937. His skill at chess kept him safe for awhile. Unfortunately for him, he was picked up by the Gestapo and sent here. I did what I could for the poor man, but in the end his body gave out. I'm sure you understand.

Before he died Brodsky told me of your prowess as a player and of your interest in the camp. I know the work you do is important, but if you could spare a little time I would consider it my personal pleasure to show you around. The camp is sixteen kilometers from Munich. Shall we say this coming week, Thursday at 10AM sharp?

The letter is signed, Adjutant Leopold Brennermann for *Kommandant, Sturmbannfuehrer* (Major) Franz Kraus.

The pencil pusher from Hamburg shows me the letter. I pretend that I have no interest in the camp, knowing the pencil pusher won't let me talk my way out of going. He reminds me how important Dachau is. Without allowing me to say another word on the matter, he instructs me on proper attire and to be ready to leave my apartment at 8AM sharp. To make sure I don't oversleep, my two protective custodians from across the street arrive at my apartment at 7AM.

The weather is sunny, bright blue skies, few clouds. The Gestapo men and I eat breakfast at a nearby inn. The Benz military car waiting for us is clean and shiny. The driver takes us along the river Amper, past an orchard of peach trees. The camp is on a hill overlooking the river. We clear several checkpoints—then drive toward a building with the death-head insignia of the SS (*Totenkopfverbände*).

Inside, I'm greeted warmly by Brennermann, the *Kommandant's* Adjutant. Short and quick in his movements he is your typical petty bureaucrat, used to making sure every detail is addressed, from papers to protocol. At precisely five minutes to ten I'm ushered into an anteroom where a chessboard and pieces have been laid out on a large table. Two high-backed chairs are on opposite sides. I stand at attention. The adjutant stands behind me also at attention.

I haven't too long to wait. *Kommandant* Kraus is punctual. He's of average height and weight, his tunic emblazoned with medals. The only thing missing from sight is his SS tattoo. He removes his cap, shakes my hand, motions me to sit and when I do sits down across from me. His thinning reddish-brown hair suggests a man in his late-fifties. His body is trim and he has a physical presence. I almost wish we were playing cards or kicking a football.

I won't bore you with details of the match. Kraus is a decent player, but not very good. I do my best to keep the game interesting. Every so often I catch Leopold Brennermann crane his neck. Kraus is so intent on the game he doesn't realize his adjutant is carefully observing his every move.

Applying the coup de grace provides me with great satisfaction—if only for the adjutant's sake. Once the match is over, we shake hands. *Sturmbannfuehrer* Kraus clicks his heels and beats a hasty retreat, while the adjutant is all smiles. I've done something it seems he'd like to do himself. He shows his gratitude by grasping my arm and leading me outside into the yard.

"What would you like to see?" he says, deferentially.

I'm not sure if I want to see anymore. From the moment I'm dropped off at SS headquarters, there's an invisible terror in the air. Worse is the death pall that hangs limply like wet wash on a clothesline. My Gestapo escorts have struck up a conversation with one of the women guards. I remember the look on Brodsky's face, the look of someone who once had a life not too different than mine. But for the rise to power of the Nazis, he might have been able to live out his life in peace.

"I should get back to my work," I say.

"There are some interesting people in one of the barracks."

"What kind of people?"

"They're Jews, but not the run of the mill type. Many of them have degrees from several universities. Did you know that Dachau was the very first camp? The Fuehrer started it in1933."

"Quite a beginning," I say laconically, adding, "It seems so long ago."

"What can last?" he says, obliquely.

I look at this man and think, what keeps him doing this kind of work without total revulsion?

"Come," he says, "I'll show you something you can tell your grandchildren about."

I'm not disappointed—but disgusted, first by the fetid smell, then by what I see, finally by what I hear—moaning, praying—double-decker iron beds filled to overflowing with the remains of human beings, skeletons hiding in baggy striped pants and ragged striped shirts. Men and women—it's hard to tell one sex from the other—waiting for their hearts to stop beating, for their lungs to stop breathing a ghastly form of insidious death.

The adjutant walks as though out for a stroll in the park. He smiles from time to time in a cadence of his own. I look at several faces, but find it hard. We walk almost the length of the barracks when I spot an old woman in one of the bunks, her head propped up by an empty sack folded over several times. I motion to the adjutant that I'd like to speak to her, adding that she was a very fine chess player. He allows me a moment of privacy and walks over to speak to an inmate, a bedbug charged with keeping the others in line. The woman looks at me and asks, "Is that you, Kurt?"

"It's me," I reply, knowing who she is.

She looks at me as if seeing a ghost. "She thought you were dead. Where have you been?"

"I've been working," I say, reluctant to explain.

"All those years she thought you were dead. What do you do?"

"I work for them. But, I'm not free."

"Do something for me if you can?"

"If I can."

"See that my demise is made swifter. This waiting to die is hard on my nerves. It isn't easy wondering if I'm going to end my life as an experiment on a doctor's table."

I can hardly bear to look at Frau Adler. She's grown old and frail, this once-powerful woman with thick legs and a broad neck. I search through my pockets and find a small package of mints. I put one into her mouth. I notice her gold teeth are gone. She says the dentist at Dachau is very efficient. She rolls the mint around in her mouth, careful not to swallow too soon. I hand her the rest. She slips it inside a tear in her foul-smelling mattress. Despite her request to be spared this life, a part of her must still have hope for salvation.

"Where is Freda?" I ask.

"Freda is with her father...in heaven."

"Did she remarry?"

Frau Adler shakes her head. "She was betrayed."

"By whom—was it Kessler?"

"She was arrested by the Gestapo. They tortured her, accused her of crimes of which she is completely innocent. Yes, and sleeping around. She was never unfaithful to your brother. There is a child, a boy."

"Alive?"

"God-willing, he's in America. The poor child found his mother in an alley—what was left of her. Can you imagine at nine and already he's sworn vengeance?"

My Gestapo friends are getting restless. They see me talking to the old Jewess and are no doubt asking themselves; why does he waste his time talking to the old sow who is scheduled to be gassed and incinerated the following week?

"I must go, Frau Adler."

Frau Adler shows her gratitude by reaching out her hand. Before touching my face she instinctively realizes her mistake. She's thinking of me, not herself when she makes the sign of the cross.

The guards look away as I walk out of the barracks. Later in *Kommandant* Kraus' office the camp commander, remembering Brodsky and how well he played, asks, "Did you find another great Jewish chess player?"

"I found one of his cousins."

"Can the Jewish sow play the game?"

I recall Frau Adler's thoughtful act in not giving me away, her brain able to function at a high level of consciousness, even under these conditions what I interpret as her mute forgiveness for the terrible things her innate intelligence tells her I've done.

"I'm afraid not."

"Then, you've made your trip for nothing. Not so?"

"On the contrary," I say, "I've learned how well we are running the camps."

"I thought your interests are more directed to the use of strategy."

"Until I came and saw for myself what goes on here I thought, disposing of a weak enemy is at best a tactical move with limited objectives. Upon closer examination, I am now of another opinion. The use of strategy in Dachau is in evidence everywhere... though I reserve judgment as to its effect on the war effort."

Kommandant Kraus' face reddens. I've gone too far. Still, I don't care. I think: Poor Frau Adler...Poor Freda.

I wonder: Why did Uncle Kurt provoke a pig as ruthless as Kraus, who fed his belly every day and got up from the table with an aftertaste of human offal? Also, Uncle Kurt's feelings for my mother go too deep, even now, after so many years. Freda was his sister-in-law. He writes as though she meant more to him. Was he in love with her? And, if so, was my father aware of his feelings?

Of course, there is a more pressing matter to be ascertained: Is the man on the other side of the ocean really Uncle Kurt?

I wrote: Your words about my grandmother Sarah are touching. The part about you giving her candy reminded me of the day I left Germany—standing on the dock in Hamburg. Just before I went aboard the ship going to America, she put a piece of chocolate in my mouth. There's something else. Tell me, please, what is it you do? There are times your words sound like those of a professor or doctor...somewhat detached from events that are going on and yet deeply concerned with what goes on in people's minds.

Also, your concern for my mother goes deeper than the feelings a man would normally have for his sister-in-law. I ask you: were you in love with her or are your feelings based on something you're not telling me?"

XIII. Buenos Aires

I didn't hear from my uncle for some time. It made me both suspicious and concerned. There were times I felt optimistic—what with the Common Market and the Euro proving money no longer needed separate beds, even if the marriage was arranged. I considered going to Germany, but each time plans were made something came up to prevent it. And, of course, there was always the question of conserving money should something turn up. The on-again off-again routine became a kind of joke in my mind. Still, it didn't make me laugh.

Then, I saw an ad in the *New York Times*. It was in the merchandise for sale section. Someone was selling a painting from the Bauhaus period in Germany. The ad said the painting was found in the attic of a house on Bank Street in the West Village.

I called, gave my name and asked a few questions. The woman at the other end said the painting was a portrait of a woman, that it had been signed, though she found herself unable to read the letters even with a magnifying glass. She said she was getting on in years and that her vision wasn't very good. She offered another reason: the bottom portion of the frame was burned.

At the time, several years before the new millennium, I thought this might be the Kessler I was looking for and made an appointment to see it that very day. What followed caught me completely off-guard. No more than an hour or so later, as I was about to leave my shop, I received a call from the same woman. She explained she'd received an offer from someone else she said wished to remain anonymous and that she'd accepted the offer. I asked her if I could make a counteroffer, should it be the painting I wanted. At this point, the woman became defensive. "If you waited all your life for a windfall, would you try to get more money than you could hope to spend in a lifetime or would you say to yourself, 'I'm a very lucky woman indeed and accept the offer?' I'm sorry, but we had no formal agreement. I have my old age to consider. Not to mention how thankful I am to God Almighty for this gift he's sent me in the form of a slender, gray-haired angel, who if truth be told, might be my older sister." After which, she hung up.

Following the somewhat bizarre turn of events, leads were scant. I remained diligent and devoted to a task that seemed hopeless until God sent another angel…one who arrived in the form of Marty Sunshine.

Bombarded by thoughts of what might lie ahead, I made myself a pot of coffee and went into my study and took another look at the black book. Leopold Brennermann kept a detailed account of what went on at Dachau. Passages referred to Bruno Schneider, but the adjutant cited no evidence that connected Schneider to my mother or her death.

I checked my e-mail. There was mail from Aldo, who wrote, Couldn't sleep, kept thinking about a picture of your father you showed me holding a chess trophy in his left hand. Did you know the letters sent to you from Germany were also written by a south-paw? I'd like to study the picture a little while longer with your permission. I put a pot of fresh coffee on. If you desire something better than the battery acid you concoct, feel free to drop in."

I was about to take Aldo up on his offer when I received an e-mail from Germany. It seemed a man had come back from the dead. Over nine years had passed since I'd heard from my uncle. It began, Dear David: No doubt my letter will come as a shock. You may even have thought me dead. The truth is I've been quite ill. The miracle is I'm alive. A man of one hundred years lives one day at a time, hopes for the best and asks for no favors. A mutual friend, Martin Sunshine, got word to me about certain matters I wish I had known about sooner. What I tell you should answer questions I previously was unwilling to answer. It's a long story. If what I'm about to say upsets you, I only ask that you hear me out before you plunge blindly ahead with whatever plans you've made.

Many interpretations have been advanced with regard to Germany's role in the subhuman Nazi culture. It is our country's shame and, while we have recovered our place among the nations of the world, we can never forget what we did as a people. Yes, it's true that everyone suffered—including Germans like me. Still, it's a weak excuse if we seek to smooth the shrouds covering bodies and ashes of the millions who died in the death camps in ways never known before to civilized humanity. I say this to you because of what I've seen, been part of, and have never been able to get completely out of my system.

In the bombed-out streets of postwar Berlin, in a sea of hollow-eyed faces, I walked alone. 'The walking wounded' is an expression you Americans use, but it's not quite accurate in this case. Berliners walked in a dream we had no choice but to live. Yet, there was a connection between all of us—if only we could talk about it. I know these people. Perhaps, they know me. Each of us so self-absorbed in our own private grief we belong to no one but ourselves.

The razed buildings coughed up a powdery smoke, behind which many hid detached as uncoupled rail cars. And, while these people did not act with the same cold-blooded detachment as an SS welcoming rail cars at the death camp depots with rifle and bayonet, there was not enough revulsion to force them to admit they knew what was happening and did nothing to make it stop happening.

In this way responsibility was blurred. They said (and some still believe) that those who invaded our Fatherland, who dropped bombs around the clock and destroyed our once-beautiful cities, are also guilty. (The firebombing of Dresden is an example, yet seldom does anyone mention the fires burning through the night, every night in the death camp furnaces) They act as though it didn't matter (during these terrible times) if the truth was distorted or that they disengaged themselves from reality, refusing to acknowledge the reasons (after Nuremberg) for our silent demeanors.

Mercifully, postwar Berlin left little time for addled minds or idle hands. There was too much work to do. As the old saying goes, *'Ohne Fleiss kein Preis.'* (Without Industriousness there is no Reward.) We rolled up our sleeves and began the arduous task of reconstruction, rebuilding Berlin by repairing broken streets, restoring monuments and buildings, regenerating pride. Everyday, I joined a battalion of men and women moving debris onto trucks. I distributed food...helped unload medical supplies for the Red Cross. I worked nights in cemeteries burying the remains of nameless people.

One day on my way to work, I saw a young boy scavenging through the rubble of a bombed-out house. He reminded me of myself as a boy—long, matted blond-hair, determined blue-eyes, ribs sunken like a wolf.

I stop reading, ask myself, am I dreaming or does it sound as though Uncle Kurt describes my father—unless they're twins? I continued reading.

Each time I passed I saw him working. With a portion of the money I earned I bought cheese, a roll and two apples and invited him to share my lunch. While we ate he told me his name was Walter Spiegel; that his father was a soldier who hadn't come home from the war and that his mother disappeared just before the last bombardment. He was afraid the Russians had taken her if she wasn't already dead. "She went out everyday to find food," he said. "One day from the upstairs window I saw her give her wedding ring to a man. I follow him. When he stops to tie his bootlace I walk ahead. As I pass him he grabs my arm, asks why I'm following him. I tell him I want to work for him so I can earn enough money to buy back my mother's ring. He laughs at me and releases my arm. When I follow him again he gives in. Three weeks later I have the ring."

"What kind of work?" I asked.

"Siphoning petrol from cars. Stealing goods from delivery trucks, whatever he tells me to do."

"I put the ring in my mother's jewelry box and hide it in a safe place in the house. The next day there's another air raid. I go to the shelter before the bombs start falling. When I come home there's nothing left of the house. My mother has still not come home. When I find the ring it will make a nice surprise for her when she does."

"Walter," I said, "why don't you finish your lunch?" He ate the cheese and apple like a bird. "I will eat the roll later," he said. "I've had enough for now." He was fifteen and looked no more than twelve. I asked myself, Why does he waste his energy looking for his mother's wedding ring? Why is this symbol of two people's love for each other so important to him? It would seem that it's buried for all time. Then, I think perhaps, he feels the symbol of their marriage belongs to him as well. Perhaps, he looks for what he once had—a father and a mother, a family.

I knew then what I wanted to do with the rest of my life. I wanted to help others understand this mysterious world in which we live. Helping Walter Spiegel find his mother's wedding ring validated my destiny yet to be. Together we moved chunks and pieces of his former life; part of a stairway leading to the upstairs bedrooms, the leg of a bed, arms of chairs, a caved in kitchen stove, the door of an icebox, burnt cotton wadding, charred and splintered floorboards, table split in two like a walnut, pieces of roof shards and slivers of wood.

On the thirtieth day, under a fragment of twisted metal, I found a small box covered with white powder. It was well-preserved considering what had come crashing down on or around it. I opened the box and took out the ring. It looked like a ring I once owned. I tried it on my fourth finger. It fit. How was that? Surely, Walter Spiegel's mother didn't have the same size fingers of a man. Perhaps, it was his father's ring that his mother saved hoping he'd return and sold when she knew he wouldn't.

Amidst the confusion, the Red Cross searching for little Walter's parents had found evidence that Walter Spiegel's father was dead, but that his mother was alive. She'd been looking for him. It would make a nice story if mother and son were reunited. Unfortunately, that was not the case. When Walter Spiegel's mother finally returned to the house, one place she managed to avoid in her 'search,' it was too late. Walter's little body had given out. He lay on a bed of straw with hands clasped holding a wedding ring. He'd fallen asleep, but would never wake up. Nevermind the late arriving mother! For her, I had no pity.

For me, there were questions I had to answer. One: Why was I so busy straightening out what seemed to me to be important work at the time—the mangled machinery of Berlin, yet hadn't found more time to look in on Walter Spiegel, to provide one human connection on which he could depend? If any good could come out of this pitiful example of neglect, it was a promise I made to myself to do better in the future.

Perhaps, the recognition of responsibility portended a reawakening of my soul. I'd been dead for so long there were times when I no longer knew my true identity. I returned to school. Ten years of long hours, tedious labor and making every penny count helped me complete my education and obtain a degree in medicine. In 1966, after additional study and psychoanalysis, I passed the necessary examinations and met the requirements. I became a licensed psychiatrist and went into private practice. I rented a small office on Marienplatz in a section of the Old Town. The following year, I received a letter from my former professor and mentor, Dr.Georg Klugman, referring a man named Samuel Greenberg, a survivor of the death camps.

Greenberg came to my office in a terrible state. I tried not to focus on his nervous mannerisms. Instead, I lighted my pipe, sat back in my chair and encouraged him to talk. He began by telling me about a recurrent nightmare about a doctor who did experiments using electricity. It was a difficult story to tell. Greenberg was sweating. When he finished he managed to tell me I'm the first doctor who didn't remind him of this maniac.

"How do you know the man is a doctor?"

"By his uniform."

I'm puzzled. Freud had written about patients who made up dreams for a variety of reasons. I knew that doctors who were party members wore uniforms, but not until I saw a photograph in a magazine of Nazi doctors in casual attire relaxing at a retreat near one of the death camps, did I feel the palpable sensation of men dancing on the graves of their victims. Weeks went by. Unable to guide my client out of his dark world, I looked at the pale, unshaven face sitting across from me and said, "I won't charge you for the time we've spent here."

"Why not?"

"I'm new at this. A more experienced man might serve your purposes better."

"I like talking to you."

I looked closely at the man as if seeing him for the first time. He had blue eyes. His course hair, mostly gray, was a brighter color when he was young, perhaps red. I was soon aware of every manifestation of his physical being, knowing my true purpose was to probe deeper.

"May I ask how old you are?"

"I'm thirty-seven."

He looked twice that age. He read my reaction and said with wry humor, "You were expecting a younger man?"

I had to keep myself from laughing out loud. His sense of self amazed me, and, of course, his sense of humor. "What kind of work do you do?"

"It's a secret."

"Everything you tell me in this room is confidential. How old were you when they came for you?"

"I was twenty-one when they took us away."

"What happened to the others?"

"I held my father's hand, but in the confusion we were separated."

"How were you separated?"

"The SS in charge carries a cane he uses like a wand. Our 'fairy godfather' looks us over like cattle. The ones he taps on the shoulder with his cane are allowed to live for as long as they can work. The ones he doesn't tap must walk ahead, knowing they are destined for the gas chambers. I work hard, drink the water no matter how bad it tastes. That's how I stay alive, one day at a time doing what I'm told; drinking the water."

"And, the rest of your family—did they drink the water too?" Greenberg shrugged his shoulders. "Did you find them—after the war?"

"I'd rather hunt."

"What do you hunt?"

"It's my job not to tell." I pointed to my chest—meaning me too. "I feel more comfortable knowing what I say is in your head as well as in mine. Perhaps, someday you can teach me how you're able to sit so relaxed in a chair, smoke your pipe and scribble notes. And, speak in a soft, persuasive voice."

I paid no attention to his attempt at humor and asked, "Did you expect him to drink the water?"

"If he wasn't thirsty, he wasn't thirsty."

"Did it make you angry?"

"Did I say I was angry?"

I began our next session differently. I told him that in 1923 I joined the Nazi Party. No reply. "My family was starving." No reply. "I went on a mission."

"Was it successful?"

"I have a son."

"What happened to him?"

"He went to America."

I couldn't help but wonder if I was that son and if he would ever acknowledge me? Or would he continue this game he plays? What could I do? I couldn't stop the flow of what he had to tell me. I had to be patient, to wait until he told me on his own terms.

"When you want to find him you'll figure out a way."

"You seem to know a great deal. Won't you share some of your knowledge with me?"

"My father could have taken my hand. I could have taken the hand of my mother, she the hand of my brother and he the hand of my sister and so on. There were eight of us."

"And?"

"We could have gone to South America."

"Why, South America?"

"Because people live in South America who did worse things than being born Jews and they live in peace."

Such is the unreasonableness of a reasonable man. I tell you this story for a reason. Samuel Greenberg or as I come to call him, 'Greenie,' becomes my friend. One reason our friendship grows is because we share. Philosophically, we share a mutual dislike for anyone with designs on improving the world solely on their terms. Greenie introduces me to his friends; Jews in Germany forced to live on the fringe because, even after the terrible slaughter, they are not accepted by many Germans.

Greenie's friends have trouble accepting me. After all, I'm not a survivor like they are, nor am I a German who swears he knew nothing of the death camps or what went on there. My open admission of what I did teaching chess to high-ranking officers doesn't win their approval. It's only when they see the change in Greenie that they view me more tolerantly.

They allow me to join their cadre. For people who came very close to being exterminated, these men breathe fire. They drink, sing, dance and when not working to earn enough money to survive, they train for missions with the determination of commandos. Each takes an oath to track down murderers responsible for the deaths of loved ones. Number one on their list are the black-shirted SS and Gestapo, loyal children of the Fuehrer, one-thousand of who are allowed to enter the United States after the war, more to scatter legally to other continents when the lights go out.

In the summer of 1967, Greenie and four hand-picked men cross the ocean by freighter to Buenos Aires. A month goes by before I find out they've run into bad luck. The men they look for have disappeared, possibly forewarned by Nazi sympathizers. A single clue leads them to a psychiatric hospital in Buenos Aires. There they find the wife of a doctor, a plastic surgeon. Greenie asks if I can fly to Argentina to interview this woman.

I rearrange my schedule and book the earliest flight I can get. Not until I'm in the air do I examine my motives. On this my first mission, I find myself possessed by vengeful thoughts. I realize the hypocrisy, having sworn an oath to heal the sick. I try, but cannot always keep these vengeful thoughts at bay. Fortunately, my rational brain has an equal say in tormenting me. By the time the plane lands I'm determined to see justice done—but not at the expense of innocent people.

Before going to see the wife, Greenie tells me her husband was one of the men they were after. The tricky part is the doctors at the hospital find her totally unresponsive, except for the few words she writes in Spanish. Her name is Sabine Van Ness.

There is no doubt in my mind that this woman is Ilse's mother, Sabine. What other secrets does this man have in store for me? I can hardly wait.

Greenie thinks it might prove useful if I can find out anything about her husband. He had a successful practice in Frankfurt before the war, kept a very busy schedule and had little interest in politics. However, once the war began to go against us many high-ranking officials in the party were observed visiting his office.

I go to the hospital, show my credentials. My cover story is that I've been asked by relatives of the Van Ness family to find out what's happened to their beloved sister, cousin and aunt. The director of the hospital receives me cordially, if a bit stiffly. Frau Van Ness' therapist, a young man in his thirties with blond hair and light complexion wearing a white coat, discusses her case with me in fluent German. He says in the short time she's been there they've made no progress, that any help I might offer would be greatly appreciated. As he shows me to her room, I can't help thinking how much he looks like a Nazi in sheep's clothing.

Frau Van Ness sits in a chair beside a window looking out at a majestic green forest. After we're introduced, the therapist takes his leave. Frau Van Ness is a plain-looking woman in her late-forties, thin and pale for this tropical climate, dressed in black. She writes in Spanish, but the remoteness of her expression suggests she lives someplace other than Buenos Aires.

I look at her and smile. There's no response. I ask her what kind of books she likes. I speak to her in German, which makes her uncomfortable. There's a book on the nightstand near her bed. I ask if I can have a look. She doesn't answer. I pick it up. "*Cien Anos de Soledad*' by Gabriel Garcia Marquez," I say, this time adding in Spanish, "I'm not familiar with his work." Still, I get no response. "It's recently been published," I say, noticing the date on the backside of the title page. She appears uneasy; I hand her the book. She takes it and puts it in her lap, laces her fingers over it. After a moment or two of silence, I tell her what a nice face she has despite her not making an attempt to highlight her beauty with makeup. No response. Before I leave the hospital I ask if she would mind if I brought a book of my own the next time I visit. At my show of a mindset she offers an almost imperceptible sigh.

I return the following day with a thin volume of the stories of Heinrich Böll. He's a personal favorite of mine, a writer whose stories are funny and poignant in an original way. I show her the book. She seems disinterested. I notice one small change in her appearance. Not her dress or makeup, but a tiny smear of lipstick. Inwardly pleased, I offer no mention of the slight alteration. Instead, I sit down in a chair near hers and open the book. I tell her I'd like to read one of the stories, but I'm not sure which one. No response. I select *The Laugher.* It's about a man who gets paid for laughing. Naturally, it's written in German.

As soon as I begin to read, Frau Van Ness averts her eyes. I maintain my concentration and continue reading. The expression on Frau Van Ness' face gradually changes. It seems she isn't deaf to German literature—just to the German language. The wry approach of a most skillful writer captures her heart in spite of herself. I wish I could report Frau Ness smiled or shed tears or did anything to indicate a change in her condition. Perhaps, another story will achieve that end. Sadly, I haven't the time.

I report my findings to Greenie. He and his men return by freighter to Germany empty-handed. On each subsequent trip I make to South America, I look in on Sabine. We become better acquainted. Still, all through the years of her confinement she remains mute.

XIV. ON OPPOSITE SIDES

I n July of 1994, I receive a call from the director of the hospital. He informs me Frau Van Ness is dying. And, the first words anyone has ever heard from her are, "I wish to see Dr. Mannheim," *auf Deutsch*. When her message reaches me, I drop everything. Before leaving Berlin, I tell Greenie, who insists on coming along to take care of transfers, annoying red-tape, and me as I'm about to celebrate my ninetieth birthday. On the plane I think of the times Sabine and I communicate without words. They're pleasant times, yet with our lengthy and complicated histories—disturbing times as well. What the medical stooges don't know is that Sabine and I have this psychic connection.

The plane takes off before Greenie asks how I feel. I tell him I never felt better. His response is that he has to look out for his mentor and good friend. Once we arrive, I leave Greenie to look up some people he knows and go to the hospital where I'm met by the new director and his staff. He's different than previous ones. He's impressed that I've come all this way—but more importantly that he's able to point to a great breakthrough in the case. "Frau Van Ness has spoken after so many, many years," he says, shaking my hand, holding it for a long time.

After a brief conversation with her therapist, a woman doctor named Flores, I'm taken in to see Sabine. She's lying in bed with her eyes closed. I approach slowly, quietly. I'm at her side when she opens her eyes. Seeing me, she smiles. I smile, too.

"How are you?" I whisper, as Dr. Flores tiptoes out.

"I feel like an old woman," she replies, in a melodic voice.

"My bones creak like an old door hinge," I reply.

"You look fine," she says, bringing her hand out from under the covers, taking hold of mine. I slide my fingers until I clasp her wrist; find her pulse steady and strong.

We don't speak until our hands grow warm. I know something I didn't know before I came into the room. Sabine isn't dying—not for a long time. I help her sit up in bed, as the nurse comes in. "I'd better tell Dr. Flores," she says, before leaving. Meanwhile, I listen to Sabine express her dissatisfaction with world conditions, how nice it is to sit and look out at the trees.

"Have you met the new director?" she asks.

"He seems different than the others."

"He's a Nazi like the rest only more clever," she says. I dare not speak. Her voice, hoarse at first, clears. She whispers, "As long as I don't say anything and they can lie to my daughters why I don't write they can't be sure of what I know. Killing me would simplify matters, but not without a price to pay. How will Carl Schneider, who is married to Trudi, my eldest, and already responsible for one death in the family, explain it? As long as I'm a prisoner at his expense I'm safe. More importantly, Trudi and Ilse are safe."

"Would you care for some water?"

"How did you know I was thirsty?"

"I'm a doctor," I reply, borrowing a page from Greenie's book of acerbic humility.

"You're a great deal like my departed husband, may God rest his soul. Stefan was a good man, the very best in his field until they forced him to do things against his will. What can a doctor do if they threaten his wife and child?"

I take several moments before answering. "I worked for them during the war. They convinced me of things that weren't true. I'm young, naïve. I believe them. I've spent the rest of my life trying to atone."

"When I'm dead I want you to have something," Sabine says. "It's a letter, an affidavit sworn to, signed by me and witnessed. There's someone who works here I can trust. What Stefan did was also accomplished with a gun to his head. Carl Schneider murdered my husband in the sanctity of his own home. I know because I saw him do it." She looks directly at me. "You're a young man in your heart and it makes my own heart glad to know there are human beings like you in the world who still believe in justice and are willing to die for it. I'm tired." I help her get comfortable, kiss her forehead and tiptoe out.

I don't visit Frau Van Ness again nor do I hear from her. As far as I know she's still alive. My only regret is that I am unable to save her from her unjust internment. Before we leave for Berlin, Greenie gets word from a reliable source that a man bearing the likeness of a man on a short list of mass murderers has been seen in the Floresta neighborhood of Buenos Aires. He's holed up inside the house he's lived in since the Nineteen-Fifties.

What Greenie, at sixty-three no longer an old-young man, doesn't know is that this day—July 18th, 1994—a plan to blow up the Jewish AMIA building is underway, that a Hezbollah suicide bomber had already entered the country by way of the Argentina-Brazil-Paraguay border triangle and is on his way to make it happen.

In a totally unrelated event, rather than wait for instructions, Greenie goes after the Nazi. I'm not sure of the details of their confrontation, but in the ensuing gun battle Greenie is fatally wounded. The man he goes after is also wounded, and both men are brought to the same hospital. In a bizarre turn of events, due to crowded conditions at the hospital (a result of the terrorist attack), they're placed side by side in beds in the same room separated only by a bamboo screen.

I arrive just before Greenie expires. I tell him he got his man. He smiles that wry smile of his and asks me to do him a favor. "Anything," I say.

"Tell Devorah I love her. Make sure she's okay." I nod my head, as life ebbs out of him.

I'm about to call for the nurse when the Nazi in the next bed, old but strong, says, "Your friend is kaput." He smiles a different smile, the kind that makes you wonder what will wipe the arrogant smirk off his face and of those like him who feel superior to others based on the life force beating in all people's bodies—their blood. With Greenie dead, I move toward the other man. I, too, smile—a friendly smile. It puts the man at ease. I prop up his pillows. He says, *"Danke schön,"* to which I answer, *"Bitte schön."*

I take a deep breath and look down at his bald pate. Inhaling as I take the top pillow, using all my strength, I press it down over his face as hard as I can. He struggles for life, but I refuse to give an inch. I keep pressing until there is no resistance. My heart pounds in my chest. I try to catch my breath. Finally, I ring for the nurse.

The hospital staff is shocked at the strange turn of events. They question me. The police question me. I tell them, "Mr. Greenberg died peacefully. The other man seemed to be having trouble breathing. I rang for help as soon as I saw that he was turning blue." They see on my passport that I'm a doctor. They look at the two men lying dead side by side; look at me, a man with all the outward manifestations of advanced age and cannot conceive that I possess the strength required to accomplish the deed.

XV. DEVORAH

The chaos created by the bombing of the *Argentine Israelite Mutual Association*—leaves me anxious, makes my leaving Buenos Aires imperative. After being quarantined for several days, during which I feel the acute symptoms as expressed by some of my patients, Argentine authorities finally allow me to leave the country with Greenie's body on board. As soon as we land in Berlin, I call a number I find in Greenie's wallet. Devorah, his wife answers. Her reaction to my news is suppressed tears and kind words for my concern. Suddenly, I feel my heart racing as if I'm being chased. I feel faint, need oxygen, am unable to walk. I have no idea how I get home.

Several days later, still a bit shaky, my driver takes me to Greenie's place. It's a small house with nothing to distinguish it from similar ones in a neighborhood where the people who live here find the modern world difficult enough without burdening themselves with unnecessary possessions.

With the aid of a cane I reach the front door, only to see it swing open as if I was expected. Devorah, wearing black, twisting a handkerchief in her raw-looking hand, cordially invites me in, takes my hat and shows me into the living room. She walks with a pronounced limp. "Are you the doctor?" she asks. I nod, watch her limp to where wooden boxes placed in front of furniture are covered with white bed sheets. "It's a Jewish custom for mourning the dead," she explains, then asks if she can bring me a chair.

"Don't go to any trouble," I reply.

"It's no trouble," she says, bringing in a wooden folding chair. "Greenie told me about you. He said you were a good man."

"Is there anything I can do?"

"He's in good hands."

"What about money?"

"His friends chipped in. I'll be all right."

"I'm sorry I wasn't at the funeral. I'm not as strong as I used to be."

"You were strong enough to take care of the man responsible."

"Who told you?"

"People who love my husband find out things. Can I bring you something to eat or drink?"

I shake my head, think of how Greenie and I, joined by others take part in shortening the distance between our diverse cultures. Beer, music and song and the day is reshaped into what life might be if we gave it a chance. "Perhaps, I can help you find work."

"I'm not able to work. I'm lucky to be alive."

"Nazis do terrible things."

"Were you one of them?"

"What makes you ask that?"

"My husband and I slept in the same bed."

I smile at her choice of words—so much like her husband's. "What else did Greenie tell you?"

Devorah walks to the window in a way that suggests that a heavy weight crushed her spine. Despite her burden she has a powerful inner force, a determination to get herself up from the bed each day onto her feet. God only knows what propels her forward. She stops; I feel myself breathe more normally. From where she's standing I see her in profile. It makes me think I've seen her before. Of course, that's impossible. I've been virtually entombed since the Gestapo first took over my life. Even after the war I live like a mole. I work, go to school, study and practice psychoanalysis. The time I spend with Greenie and his buddies, the trips to South America is the sum total of my 'worldly' experience.

While these thoughts go through my mind, I see that the woman is crying. Something—a thought or remembrance affects her. I feel as though I'm intruding on her grief. "I should go," I say, getting to my feet. "Please, don't hesitate to call if you think I can be of service," I add, leaving my card on a table. "I, too, lost someone very dear to me."

"Was her name Freda?"

"How did you know?" She doesn't answer.

Of course, in the same bed again. "The woman bore you a son, didn't she?"

Why does he continue to write to me in this manner? Still, what choice do I have except to read on?

"It's another reason why I owe your husband so much."

"Why is that?"

"He helped me find my son."

My eyes ask for more.

"I can't continue until I tell you who I am; that is if you haven't guessed by now. I am your father, Ernst Mannheim. I would like to continue in order to provide you with an accurate account of what went on and how best to handle the situation you find yourself in—hopefully not because of anything I've done. It would be too ironic to have done what I could to spare you, only to find out I've led you into a trap. I wait anxiously for your reply."

At first, I felt nothing. He had a mission. I had a mission.

He was tortured until he convinced those who wanted to use him that he would do his part. I tortured myself until the day I met Ilse. It seemed to me that he was seeking to redeem himself in my eyes. I had my own ideas of redemption, and no desire to give in to him. How could I accept his words? No, I won't accept them...the words of a man who denied his only child what a loving father would offer. The fact that he could be so cruel as to keep his love from me. Yet, his pseudonymous letters did keep me afloat. I could have easily drowned having made a promise I had no chance of fulfilling. Not knowing what to say, I said nothing.

I may as well tell you the rest. It's a long story, but I'll be as brief as I can. Know this if you know nothing else. I'm not looking for sympathy, David. I'm looking to help save your life. Why? Because your life means more to me than anything else.

He continued. Devorah says, "Maybe, you better sit down."

"What about you?"

"Sitting hurts." She goes to the kitchen, brings back two bottles of cold beer.

She hands me one. I take a sip. "My sessions with Greenie evolve into something more than therapy once I offer my life as proof Nazis come in many shapes, sizes and colors. And, transference begins to develop circularity."

"I'm not sure what you mean."

"What I mean is Greenie no longer saw me as a doctor but as a man much like himself, an imperfect being. It led us into uncharted territory, but it worked to our mutual benefit. I got more than the satisfaction of helping another person help himself. It gives Greenie a satisfaction usually reserved for the therapist."

"How brave of you."

"After the war I tried to find my son without success. One

minute he was alive; the next I hadn't a clue where he was or how to find him. America is a big place."

"What year did he get lost to you?"

"1933. Ten years later, before his grandmother died, she told me he was safe in America."

"He was lucky to get away."

"The funny thing was he vowed to get the ones who killed his mother."

"What's funny?"

"He was a boy, only nine years old."

Devorah shook her head. "He grew up sooner than was intended."

"You have great compassion."

"Go on, finish your story."

Greenie opened a door in my mind that had been closed. He asked if anyone in Freda's family had relatives living abroad. I told him I didn't know of any. My mother said we had no living relatives. I checked old records under Adler, Freda's maiden name, but got nowhere. One day, Greenie asked, "What was Herr Adler's occupation?" I told him he was a Professor of Physiology at the University of Berlin.

Suddenly, I knew what to do. I rushed over to the Ministry of the Interior. Many of the city's school records were either destroyed in the bombings or moved to the country. Of those that remained I found out that in 1925 Erich Menard and Paula Giroux, both US citizens, had been enrolled in one of Dr. Adler's classes. With that, I was able to find a couple living in Boston, Massachusetts that fit their description. Early in 1968, I wrote to them using my brother's name Kurt instead of my own. I received a letter back saying they'd adopted and raised a child who'd lost both parents fighting the Nazis, living in New York

City and had taken their surname; Menard. Now known as David Menard.

"Might I ask why you lied after all those years of looking for your son? Why didn't you just identify yourself as his father?"

"It's a good question. I'm not sure I know the answer. Maybe, I was afraid how a boy might respond to a father who failed to find those responsible for his mother's death. Who did what the Nazis told him to do and sometimes believed his mother was a whore."

"He's not a boy any longer."

"That's right. He's a grown man. Can I tell a grown man his father was so easily persuaded, that since finding out the truth from Frau Adler, before she was gassed and incinerated at Dachau, that model of Nazi efficiency, where they didn't kill as many as they killed at other death camps. Yet still they killed, fouled the air with the stench of burning flesh that no matter how hard I try, I can't get the stench out of my hair, my clothes, my nostrils and my mind."

"Take it easy, Dr. Mannheim," Devorah said. "Drink a little beer." I drink. 'Please, if you're able, continue."

"What if I tell him the truth about myself? What if he doesn't accept me? What is the truth anyway? What if I hide the truth from myself? It's possible and I'll tell you why," I drink a little more.

"Drink, there's plenty."

"Since I met Greenie I've felt history tugging at my sleeve. How could I accomplish what I set out to do and keep the boy, excuse me, a grown man out of it? You see I too swore vengeance."

"Never mind. You must tell him the truth as best you can, how you became part of a group who track down and catch these murdering beasts. How you killed one with your own hands. Tell him. He'll be proud of you."

Who was this Ernst Mannheim? I did my best to follow his words through all the twists and turns. Still, I felt more for Devorah Greenberg than for this displaced person who suddenly wanted to complicate my life.

I reply, Your belated revelations arrive too late. Are you so blind you can't see what you've done? Are your excuses so filled with yourself and your own life that you cannot see what I might still do with mine? Even if I had some feelings for the man who once wrote letters I came to enjoy and looked forward to receiving, the fact that you stopped writing for nine years speaks volumes of how selfish you are.

Response, I don't blame you for feeling the way you do. I know I've failed as father, as a husband, perhaps even as a man. What's important isn't what happened to me or even how it happened. What's important is how it can help you. Please, I beg you, don't dismiss what I am about to say.

In the pre-dawn hours, my eyes closing from lack of sleep, I continued reading. In 1994, having returned to Berlin without realizing the severity of my condition, I suffered a complete nervous collapse. Devorah Greenberg, even as she mourns her husband's death, locates a psychiatrist friend of mine whose name I can't remember. He suggests a sanatorium near Munich. The idea of the trip fills me with trepidation, but I agree to go. A week of tests, intensive psychotherapy and medication bring no improvement.

My doctor suggests using a technique they've had success with in similar cases—called "sleep therapy." They put me 'out' for two weeks, believing the rest will help my nerves, that when I awaken I'll be in a better frame of mind. Instead, I wake agitated, disconnected. They repeat the procedure. However, when they inject the anesthetic, for some reason my eyes stay open. I hear the chief surgeon raise his voice in a panic before I go under. I don't hear another voice until I regain consciousness nine years later. I won't go into the countless hours therapists spent trying to help me regain a portion of my former self. After all, I am now a man of one hundred years. If it wasn't for Devorah's stubborn compassion and the grace of God, I would not be alive.

David, I wish I knew sooner how deeply involved you were with the Schneiders. I say this not as your father, but as a man who knows what these swine are like. Maybe, if I had known we were after a similar justice I would have felt compelled to press you into service rather than having tried to protect you.

Reply: That's quite a story. Hard to believe actually, but I'm trying.

Response: There's an aspect of life I've never understood. Perhaps, you can help me. If a man is convicted of a crime he didn't commit or is falsely connected to some wrongdoing, oftentimes there seems to be nothing he can say or do to remove the dark cloud hanging over his head. I put myself into that dubious category. While in plain medical terms I've been in a coma.

With the aid of doctors, therapists, Devorah and loyal friends, I've progressed to where I'm able to dress and feed myself, talk, and with some help walk and write. I'm back in Berlin, but not at the old address.

Before you ask why Devorah didn't write, having been the driving force behind my belated admissions, I can only surmise she felt the tenuousness of my condition would offer no reward —not even to a long lost son—venturing from the United States to Germany and back with any degree of regularity.

Reply: I'm sorry to hear about your illness and glad you're recovering. Devorah sounds like a special person. In your last letter to me you mentioned Frau Van Ness. As you must know from Marty, Ilse Van Ness and I are good friends.

Response: I heard Frau Van Ness speak glowingly of Ilse. What makes a person trust another? Is love a sound recommendation? Put your best efforts into making sure Ilse isn't leading you into a trap, for there are strong indications she's working with the other side.

He didn't trust my mother, yet wanted me to do the same with the woman I loved. Didn't he see the likelihood of my defeat if I followed his path?

He wrote: Bruno Schneider, like so many other Nazis, was never convicted or charged with committing war crimes. Therefore, he was free to come and go as he pleased. He left Germany in 1945 with his wife and child and settled in Argentina. One of the reasons he avoided the tribunal's justice was there were no clear photographs of him and scant evidence incriminating him at Nuremberg.

If the photos taken by Leo Brennermann are in your possession and they could find their way to me it would be damning evidence. With Sabine's sworn statement testifying to Carl Schneider's guilt the two will be enough evidence to hang him. I think to myself: And, what if it isn't?

I stared bleary-eyed at the roll of film. Before answering my father's e-mail, I lay down on my bed. Light filtered in through the worn shades. I closed my eyes, but soon realized I was too tense to sleep. I walked across the hall, knocked on Aldo's door.

"What happened to you last night? I know—Ilse. Wish I had an Ilse in my life. What gets you up so early on this gloomy Friday?" Plowing straight ahead, Aldo asked, "How's about a cup of coffee and a piece of homemade Italian cheesecake? "My mother made it," he said, with some pride. I nodded, said, "Then, she's forgiven you."

"She's been talking to the priest. I think it's a good sign," Aldo said, cutting a piece. "She's from the old school. Her exercise is walking to the market every day to carefully select food." Aldo poured the coffee. I took a bite of the cheesecake. "Now, tell me what's on your mind."

"This is very good."

"I'll give you the recipe. What's up?"

I showed Aldo the roll of film, asked if he could develop the pictures right away. Aldo looked at the roll. "Its 35mm…It may take awhile."

"How long?"

"Maybe, an hour. Would you care to join me?"

I'd gone into Aldo's 6x8 darkroom once before and felt claustrophobic. "Check out this new equipment," Aldo said, snapping on a red lamp, adding, "I don't think your uncle is who he says he is. This sounds crazy, but I think he might be your father."

I patted Aldo on the back, went into the kitchen and had the rest of his cake and coffee. I called to Aldo that I was going to check my snail mail. Aldo didn't answer. Aldo was an 'original,' someone who was unaware of how much his well-rounded mind was needed in our one-dimensional world. I walked down the flight of stairs and opened the mailbox. It was empty. On my way up the stairs I heard a sound I didn't like. I called out in a voice fraught with angst, "Aldo," and took the stairs as fast as I could.

The door was ajar as I burst into Aldo's apartment. I looked for my friend… found him face down on the floor of the darkroom. He'd been shot. I turned him over and saw where the bullet entered his brain, the left temple. I pried his clenched fist open, empty!

I played with the idea that the killer didn't have time to get away, that he might still be in the apartment. I wanted my gun to even up the odds, but realized that by then he'd get away. I carefully searched the apartment, went out the door into the hall. At the top of the stairs, I saw a gray-haired woman on her way down. She didn't seem in any hurry. I thought of calling to her, but didn't want the sound of my voice to frighten her. As for Aldo, I could only think he'd been mistaken for me. It wasn't a good feeling.

When I was able I called the police, gave them the address, the apartment number and Aldo's full name. Then, I left the building as fast as I could. I needed to find a few answers. During my career as a bookbinder, I handled the work that came my way. Word of mouth from satisfied clients was all it took. There were times when the overly grateful ones suggested I advertise or promote myself more, but I was content to follow my own footprint rather than wear larger shoes. Aldo was like that—a brother.

The cab pulled to the curb. I got in, gave the driver Ilse's address and let my body sink into the hard vinyl. I was about to call Ilse when my phone rang. "Hello," a woman's voice said.

"Ilse?"

"Gisele, Carl's secretary from the gallery."

"Yes, of course the photographer."

"You remember me. Isn't that sweet?"

"What do you want?"

"Carl and I are kaput. You understand?" Gisele had been drinking. I hoped her lips might be loose enough to slip. "It happens to the best of us."

"I'm not the best. I'm a stinker. If I could I'd stick a knife in Carl's belly."

"What's he done?"

"Don't you know he's shacked up with your girlfriend, Ilse? Very sexy. Want the address?"

"Why are you telling me this?"

"I'm going home to Sweden. Mama understands. Also, my rent is in arrears—Carl's way of telling me it's over. Then, there's plane fare and presents for mama who will welcome me with open arms and many tears. Doesn't it break your heart?" She paused. "No? It breaks mine. But, after all the money I've sent her she should be nice to her only daughter who loves her...Oh, and cab-fare."

"How much for the letters?" I asked, leading Gisele on.

"I think ten thousand dollars is a fair price."

"Are we talking about Carl's copy or yours?"

"I'm a bitch. I burned Carl's copy."

"I think not, Gisele. And, Ilse's not with Carl."

"How can you be sure? Are you willing to take the chance?"

"Bye, Gisele. Be nice to mama."

"Why are you so cheap? You're a Jew. That's it, a filthy, stinking..."

By the time I got to Ilse's place, I felt better. Seeing Ilse would help. We'd have a quiet supper, get to bed early. In the morning I'd e-mail my father, tell him I no longer had the film, that it was gone along with my best friend, killed by Carl or one of his henchmen, that the reason I didn't mention it was because I wanted to capture Bruno Schneider alive and dispose of him my own way.

I rang the doorbell. There was no answer. I was about to try again when the merry-go-round sounded. "Hi," the voice said. "Where are you?"

"I'm over at Carl's." She doesn't say Carl and Trudi's—just Carl's.

"We're invited tomorrow night for cocktails."

"What time?"

There was a pause, Ilse got back on. "Sixish."

"Sounds okay," I said, puzzled.

"Trudi wants to show me the dress she's picked out for the opening. You know, girl talk. I'll just grab a bite if that's all right?"

"I thought we'd spend the evening together."

"Plenty of time for that later," she said.

"Sure, plenty of time," I replied, not meaning a word of it.

XVI. Making Plans for the Next War

Police cars, flashing lights and neighbors I barely knew. The circus aspect of New York City was never more evident than in a milling crowd waiting for the TV cameras to arrive. A police officer stopped me at the entrance and asked for some form of ID. I took out my wallet, showed him a credit card. The officer matched my name to a list of tenants and allowed me to enter.

Seeing the stairs cordoned off, I took the elevator, was met by a detective in plainclothes. The detective, a slender man with gray eyes, followed me into Aldo's apartment. The Chief was on the phone with the medical examiner. By the look on his face a Friday homicide before the weekend wasn't sitting well on his stomach.

As soon as Chief Braden was off the phone, the detective whispered something in his ear. Braden asked me my name and where I'd been. I said I went for a walk to clear my head. The detective asked what my relationship was to the deceased. I said Aldo and I were friends, that we had a cup of coffee together a few hours ago.

"What time was that, Mr. Menard?" Braden asked.

"Nine. I went to get my mail. On my way upstairs I heard a sound I didn't like."

"What kind of sound?"

"It sounded as if Aldo was in trouble."

"What were his exact words if you don't mind?" the detective asked, taking out a pad and pen.

"I really couldn't tell."

"Then, how did you know he was in trouble?"

"It sounded that way."

"You touch anything?" Braden asked. I shook my head. "Then, what did you do?"

"The door was open so I came inside. I found him lying on the floor in the darkroom."

"What made you go into the darkroom?" the detective asked. He was a man in his fifties, with sandy hair.

"He wasn't anywhere else. When I got over the shock, I called 911," I said, gasping for air.

"Maybe, you ought to lie down, Mr. Menard."

I shook my head. Braden wasn't much older than his lieutenant, with wavy black hair and deep lines in his forehead.

"Are you retired?" the detective asked.

"No."

"What do you do for a living?"

"I'm a bookbinder."

"Don't machines take care of that?"

"For the most part."

"What's the story?"

"I have a small but loyal clientele."

"Do you mind if I ask how old you are?"

"I'll be eighty in June."

"Has anyone ever told you that you look pretty damn good for your age?"

"Some days I feel pretty damn good. This isn't one of them. Is that all?"

"As a matter of fact, it isn't. Do you mind showing us what's in your wallet?"

"I just did that."

"Do it again, if you don't mind, Mr. Menard?"

"We're trying to find out who killed your friend," the Chief said.

"Sorry," I said, handing over my wallet. The detective went through it carefully and returned it.

"One more thing. You know anyone who'd like to see your friend dead?"

"I don't," I said, unwilling to bring the police any closer to what I felt was a private matter.

Before allowing me to leave, Braden recited the speech he gave Ilse—"Don't go anywhere or do anything different from your normal routine without letting us know."

Once inside my apartment, I e-mailed my father. They killed a good friend of mine and took the roll of film. I have the black book and a note from an old friend of yours.

Reply: Leopold Brennermann was never my friend. What does the note say? Can you translate German into English?

Response: My parents hired a private tutor to teach me German, thinking I might want to return to Germany someday. From what I can make out, the book seems to be a daily account of what went on in Dachau. Leo describes what you know already—the incident in the furnace room when a Jew pushed Bruno Schneider.

Reply: The problem we face is not that these beasts existed, but that they and their progeny still exist. It's vital you find a safe place for the Brennermann evidence. I know you're not used to this kind of turmoil, David. My advice is to try to remain calm.

Answer: Don't worry about me. You had your chance to offer fatherly advice thirty-six years ago.

Reply: I'm sorry, David. I neglected my duties as a father. But, you also had opportunities to tell me what you were after. As I said before, had you done that I might have responded differently. At this point it makes no sense to blame. There's too much to be done and not much time—that is if you want to see these swine punished as much as I do.

Response: You can be sure I'll do my best to make that happen. I sent Brennermann's note.

Reply: Leo Brennermann's account of what happened that day at Dachau is vital evidence. Still, we need the original copy of the note and signature in court. The photos would lend further credibility, but I fear they no longer exist. Though I have lived most of my life alone, I would never have found Sabine Van Ness on my own. Don't forget how you're accepted into Bruno Schneider's world. With the help of Sabine's daughter, Ilse, isn't it? I ignored my father's reference to Ilse.

Response: Being a great strategist on the chessboard, I think you'll appreciate the moves I intend to make.

Reply: Don't be foolish, David. Let me send someone, trained personnel. Don't you see your introduction to Ilse happens because they're anxious to find out what you know? She works for them because she believes her mother is being well taken care of in a hospital in Argentina. It isn't true. Sabine is a prisoner who sacrifices each day of her life for her daughters by not opening her mouth other than to eat barely enough food to stay alive. Remember this: her affidavit, sworn to and witnessed, and Brennermann's note, can put the hangman's noose around both Bruno and Carl Schneider's necks.

Response: Do you really think I'm counting on seeing them brought to trial?

Reply: What can I say to dissuade you—that I should have been a better example? Agreed! But, once my feet were planted in the soil of my existence I could only be a good example if and when my son found out what was in my heart. I've deprived you of such knowledge except for the letters. Even then I pretended to be someone else. You have a legitimate right to be angry especially if you feel I've deprived you of the filament of truth most sons seek from their father's, one that is supposed to shine from sunrise to sunset.

From the first day I learned you were alive I thought of you. When I discovered where you were, that I could write to you, it gave me the opportunity to say what was in my heart. Still, there was my work, important work. I had to decide whether I should spend the rest of my life in a two-pronged assault on those who killed my beloved Freda by going after the ones responsible and still have time to help the victims of the Nazi atrocities, or tell my son who I am, what I do, that I'm not just a psychiatrist listening to people's problems, but also a member of a group that hunts Nazis, and if they don't put up too much of a fight or take their own lives, brings them to trial. Yes, and also kills in cold blood if there's no other choice. I ask myself: If I revealed my identity, would you join me in my fight? In that case, I'd be responsible for what happened to you, wouldn't I?

My life as told to you by my younger brother Kurt—who died on the Eastern Front in the retreat from Stalingrad doing what he thought was his duty —seemed like a better approach. I could then tell you stories about your mother, what our life was like during those terrible times without emotion blurring things. Isn't it possible to love an uncle as much as a father? I ask you for your help in the grave matter facing us. What happens to the Mannheim's is small compared to our struggle against these aberrant criminals. In truth, David, do we not sail the same lonely sea?

Despite my negative feelings I am moved by my father's words, especially when he speaks of 'sailing the same lonely sea.'

Response: For all your maneuvering and deception your words affect me, almost as if they'd come from my own brain. It's why the letters from your alter ego were so seductive. That said there doesn't seem to be time for any lasting non-aggression pact. You have the life you've made for yourself. And, so have I.

Reply: I don't think you realize the danger. Bruno Schneider must be afraid the authorities are closing in—why else the sudden rash of killings? There have been others besides Marty who infiltrated this 'Nazi cell' only to be discovered and summarily executed by a single bullet to the left temple. Does that ring a bell?

Response: It rings a number of bells. But, that's for the authorities to deal with. Tomorrow is my chance.

Reply: Sometimes I played chess blindfolded, in which case I had to pay close attention to moves and countermoves without actual sight of them. I am not Nostradamus. However, I was a very good chess player. Remember this; The Fatherland, knowing it had lost the so-called 'Great War,' was already making plans for the next one. On their retreat through France and Belgium, German soldiers were ordered to destroy particular industries. These men didn't know the purpose or significance of what they were being asked to do nor did they care. They were simply following orders. But, there was a method to this madness, a process underway to reinvent the truth, no matter how long it took, no matter how many men were sacrificed to achieve its end.

Plans like these are presently in place—fifty, a hundred years from now. We must never lose sight of this 'Master Plan' and how sedulous these smooth-talking, well-dressed and immaculately clean ape-men are and what we can do to prevent the Nazi from once again throwing a dark shadow over the pages of history with what he envisions will be a far more favorable ending.

On a more personal note, tell me if you will, does Ilse know who killed her father?

Response: She thinks Israeli's did it.

Reply: Sabine said Carl Schneider killed her husband.

Response: It doesn't matter.

Reply: It matters. Did you mention my name?

Response: Only if you still go by the name of Uncle Kurt.

Reply: That's too bad. I'm a good friend of her mother's, as you know from our recent correspondence.

Response: So?

Reply: Does she love you?

Response: Yes.

Reply: Don't wait until you're backed into a corner. Tell her as soon as possible. Give her time to make up her mind. If she begins to doubt them, to question them, she may make a move that trips them up. Pawns can't be taken lightly, but the Queen has power.

My staff has been alerted to be on the lookout for anything that moves in your direction. It's late and you must be exhausted. I know I am. You can reach me at any hour. I've included my cell number.

There was no response. I memorized the number and destroyed any record of it.

XVII. TRUSTING ILSE

ather than intrude on Ilse's balancing act, I ate dinner alone at my favorite Chinese restaurant and walked home in the rain. From the moment I entered my apartment my mind was too active for me to sleep. I sat at the computer putting down a few thoughts of my own.

Eventually, I wrote, Despite what you say about Ilse...despite what common sense tells me is true...despite the age-old stories of men fooled by the seductive charms of women...I willingly trust her. That is, I'm willing to take the consequences if I'm wrong.

A second one, Tell me one story that you've been saving, one that stands out from all the others.

I sent the messages, went to the lavatory, opened the medicine chest and took out a plastic vial labeled, "Take one at bedtime or much more if you want to sleep a lot longer. It was signed: Dr. Aldo Antonucci." I put the vial back, went into the kitchen and drank a glass of water. I needed a good night's sleep and was about to get into bed when the phone rang.

"I'm sorry about today," Ilse said.

"So am I."

"Carl and Trudi have been very good to me."

"Have they?"

There was a pause. "Have you changed your mind about tomorrow?"

"What do you think?"

"Don't you realize what could happen?"

"Don't you?"

"Carl is in a strange mood."

"How would you feel if I were to suddenly disappear or perhaps even be abducted by Israelis?"

"Don't be ridiculous."

"Tell me I have nothing to worry about. Can you do that for the man you say you love?"

"I can tell you that Carl made it very clear that I bring you along."

"That works for me," I said, with false bravado, adding: "What do you think?"

"Why won't you listen? What can I say to make you understand?"

"Say something that doesn't predict my demise."

"There's no use talking to you. I'm going to bed."

"Make sure you double-lock your doors."

"Why do you do this to me?"

"Are you feeling regretful?"

Ilse began to cry.

"Have you heard about Aldo?"

"What about Aldo?"

"He's dead—murdered in his apartment."

"David, how awful...When?"

"Earlier today. Someone put a bullet into his left temple."

Ilse stopped crying. When she got back on her voice sounded different. "Do they know who did it?"

"If they do, they're not sharing their knowledge with me."

"You think Carl did it, don't you?"

"What do you think, Ilse?"

"What time did it happen?"

"About 9:30 this morning."

"Carl was..." Ilse hesitated.

"Were you about to say that Carl was with you?"

"How did you know?"

"I thought Gisele was lying...How naïve of me?"

"Gisele is a tramp."

"And, what are you?"

"I wasn't sleeping with Carl. I've never slept with Carl."

"Where were you and Carl at 9:30 in the morning?"

"We were at the gallery. I was helping him locate several of Trudi's older paintings."

"Isn't that Trudi's job?"

"My sister gets nervous whenever she's about to show her own work. Ordinarily Gisele would have helped, but Carl fired her."

"That seems a strange thing to do before an important show."

"Gisele has been drinking again. Carl told her to visit her mother in Sweden and get herself together or not bother to come back."

"An all-expense paid trip?"

"I don't know...Maybe."

"Where does Carl get the money? He pays for Gisele, for your mother's care... Perhaps, he helps pay your rent too?"

"Is that so bad?"

"I think it is."

"Things aren't always as they appear."

"Then, tell me how things are behind appearances?"

"I can only tell you that I love you very much. My darling David, don't you know that? Don't you feel...?"

"Not when you hide things from me and defend Carl."

"What makes you think I know everything?"

"What are you trying to say, Ilse?"

"I know very little about my mother except for the occasional letter I receive from her therapist or from the Director of the institution where she's confined."

"Why don't you take a trip down there sometime and see for yourself?"

"I'd like to, only I'm afraid. Mostly I'm afraid for Trudi, but for me as well."

"I might be able to help you."

"What is it that you have against him?"

"What do I have? I have the word of Dr. Ernst Mannheim."

"Who?"

"My father, Ernst Mannheim."

"How is it you never mentioned him before?"

"Because until recently I thought he was dead. It's a long story, Ilse, one you don't need to hear right now."

"I'm so tired, David."

"Go to bed, Ilse. Tomorrow will be a better day. Go to sleep and dream of a better day."

"Will you dream of the same day?"

"I'll do my best," I said, fully aware I'd given Ilse something the Schneider's wanted to know. That I'd taken another calculated risk, one that depended on Ilse loving me more than her own flesh and blood.

Once I was off the phone I walked into the bathroom, opened the medicine chest. I was about to take out the pills Aldo left for me when there was a knock at the door. I went to see, called, "Who is it?"

"Russ Turner."

"Sorry, I have no business hours on the weekend."

"It's Detective Turner—about Mr. Antonucci." The containment in the detective's voice suggested something important.

I cautiously opened the door. The detective with the easygoing manner stood there, his sandy hair glistening beneath the fluorescent hall light, his raincoat dripping onto the carpet. "Come in," I said, "Pardon the appearance."

"I know it's late."

"What can I do for you, detective?"

"Call me, Russ."

"It's ten o'clock at night, Russ."

"I happened to be in the neighborhood."

"Where do you live?"

"Maspeth," Turner said, rubbing his hands together.

"Can I get you something? Here, let me have your coat."

"I'm good," the detective said, taking off his coat and handing it to me.

I hung the detective's wet coat on a hangar in the bathroom shower. "I'm sorry about your friend. I know what it's like to lose a buddy," Turner said, when I returned.

"Where was that?"

"'Nam."

"You're not old enough."

"I was young when I joined, old when I got out."

"What made you choose police work?"

"I got used to always being in attack-mode."

"You don't look the part. Sit down."

"Don't mind if I do. I've been on my feet most of the day." Turner sat in the chair Aldo liked. I flinched. "I'm sorry. Is it your chair?"

"Aldo's. Don't get up. I'll get used to it."

"I'm not sure why, but I have the feeling you blame yourself for what happened."

"You're smart, Russ."

"So how come I'm only a lieutenant?" he asked jokingly.

"Perhaps, there's something you need to accomplish before you're promoted."

"Could be, David...all right if I call you—?"

"That's my name. Your captain looks like he's about ready for retirement."

"It's just his way. Some people can't resist testing the water even if they know it's too cold. People your age, meaning no disrespect, are usually winding down. From where I'm sitting I'd say you still have a pretty healthy interest in the opposite sex."

"How can you tell?"

"The way you move...what you don't say."

"I live alone."

"Ever have visitors?"

"All the time."

"Bull."

"Okay, so I don't have many friends—anything wrong with that?"

"The woman, does she have a name?"

"Don't you know her name—you seem to know a great deal?"

The detective laughed. "Now you're talking."

"I wouldn't say that."

"What would you say? Don't answer, David. Your lawyer would call it a loaded question."

"What lawyer?"

"The one you're going to need."

I got to my feet—slowly. "Mind if I pour myself a drink?"

"Only if you don't offer to pour one for me."

"What's your pleasure?"

"Whatever you're having." I set out two whiskeys. We drank up. I poured another. "You have some time?"

"At my age the days are dwindling to a precious few."

"Isn't that from a song?"

"I think it is."

"To set the record straight about my going to 'Nam, someone, who shall go nameless, forged my birth certificate."

"What do you know, an honest cop?"

"I was seventeen when I enlisted."

"How was it?"

"Not what I expected."

"You don't have to talk about it. At least you came back unscathed."

"You think so? What bothers me is I never got it straight with my old man. We didn't see things the same way. I thought I'd come home the conquering hero. His letters condemned the war. He said that we'd been had. He marched with the anti-war people, but spent most of his free time gathering evidence to support his belief that companies like Dow Chemical and General Electric were evil and dangerous. By the time my tour of duty was over, I had a few questions of my own. It would have been great to share some of those thoughts with him, but he had an accident."

"What happened?"

"Heart attack running from 'the pigs'—his words not mine—at a peace rally that turned into a riot."

"That's too bad."

"At least he lived his life the way he wanted to. He wasn't fooled by anyone."

"You think I'm being fooled?"

"Could be."

"Want some more cheap whiskey?"

"Bring it on."

I refilled both glasses. I looked at my guest differently. This wasn't just a cop. This was a man with stuff on his mind. Maybe, stuff not so different from the stuff that bothered me. Turner leaned his head back. "My father taught me something you might find interesting. It's about connecting." I wasn't sure where he was headed. Turner continued. "He had this idea about books, not just any book, but books that made you think. He said you can connect ideas from one book to another, ideas that stick in your mind or connect to a piece of music that lingers; or to a quality you've observed. He said great philosophers, all of whom made sure to let the world in on their own pet theories, had more in common with each other than they were willing to admit, that there's an overlapping interconnection. He said if something made me think, I should file it away in my brain for future use; if the idea came up in some other context, to connect the parts that overlapped or furthered the idea, in that way developing a philosophy of my own."

"Sounds deep."

"It is," Turner said, looking at me with soulful eyes.

He was talking about roads I never traveled on for fear of being diverted from my singular direction. "You must find that type of thinking useful in your work."

"I could tell you how, if you have a minute." I nodded, drank.

"The night Kyle Charlton was murdered I watched him on 'Charlton Chats.' I was totally blown away by the way he and Marty Sunshine spoke to each other. Damn it, it bothered the hell out of me. Did you happen to catch the show?"

"I did."

160

"What was your take on it?"

"It seemed provocative."

"They made nice at the end, as if nothing happened, as if they were merely flexing their intellectual muscles."

"I wasn't watching that closely," I lied.

"Sunshine was a POW in 'Nam," Turner said, "I'd almost forgotten his story—how he was captured, tortured, repatriated. How he admitted things against us which he later denied. On the show, Sunshine seemed in good spirits, yet there was something dark about what he said that suggested otherwise." I didn't answer. "Am I boring you?"

"Not at all."

"Looking through our files I found evidence that put things into perspective. Sunshine dropped off our radar until 1983 when he showed up at a protest rally of correction officers looking for better pay and safer working conditions. In case you don't know these men transport prisoners to and from courthouses pretty much on their own. What got my attention was seeing Marty Sunshine of all people standing side-by-side with a bunch of skinheads. His message was, if you can believe it, strong leadership and a dollar paid for a dollar earned. The only thing missing was the swastika armband and 'Heil Hitler salute.' Fortunately, some of us arrived before the two groups went ballistic."

"You think Marty Sunshine is a Nazi?"

"In *One World* he talks at length about the advantages of strong leadership and personal integrity while denigrating those who can't measure up. He's against programs that help people who can't afford medical insurance, who can't find a decent job and who rely on some support from the government until they find work."

"How do you think Charlton fits in with such issues?"

"He doesn't."

"I'd agree."

"What if he was, shall we say, led astray?"

"Kyle Charlton?" I said, shaking my head and swallowing my whiskey.

"What about Marty Sunshine?"

"That's hard for me to say."

"How well do you know him?"

"I once bound a book for him."

"On what subject?"

"It was an album of memories for his parents, about their life in Germany."

"Were they Holocaust survivors?"

"They were Germans, not Jews."

"Did you meet them?"

"No. Marty supplied the pictures, letters and memorabilia."

"How long is it since you and Ilse Van Ness visited Charlton's beach house?"

A torpedo shot out of the blue. "We were there yesterday," I replied coolly.

"One honest answer, shall we try for two?"

"I take it you want to know why."

"You take it correctly."

"We went there hoping to find some reason why Kyle Charlton was murdered."

"Did you find what you were looking for?"

"Not a thing."

"Would you like to try again?"

I had to be careful; Turner was onto me. There was an uncomfortable pause. Finally, I said, "Do you carry a lie detector in your pocket?" I hesitated, adding, "I'm sorry, I can't tell you anymore."

"You could be in danger."

"At my age, what's to worry?"

"Is it that you feel you can't trust me?"

"I appreciate the fact that you've been open about yourself and what you do. Frankly, I've never spoken to a police officer like you before."

"Thanks, but I'm not fishing for compliments. I'm trying to get to the bottom of a rash of killings. And, I kind of like you, David."

"Thanks, Russ. I kind of like you too."

"What if I tell you I think your paying Mr. Antonucci a visit at nine in the morning was a little early for a couple of night owls who might have trouble sleeping? I checked the medicine chest in Mr. Antonucci's apartment. Shall I check yours or would you prefer I get a search warrant?"

"No need. I do have some trouble falling asleep, but whiskey not sleeping pills is more to my liking."

"Why the early wake up call?"

"Like you said, I couldn't sleep."

"And?"

"That's all."

"No good, David. I think maybe you found a piece of film out at Kyle Charlton's beach house and asked Mr. Antonucci to develop it. The lab found traces of cellulose acetate on the fingers of Mr. Antonucci's hands. Since there isn't anything connecting Mr. Antonucci to the crime, I'd say the killer was most likely after you and may have mistakenly stumbled on Mr.—"

I broke in. "His fucking name is Aldo, Russ. He wasn't involved in any of this."

"Angry, aren't you?"

"Damn right I'm angry."

"Go on."

"You'd like that wouldn't you?"

"Try me."

"Whatever was on the film is gone."

"But, you know who wanted it enough to kill for it, don't you?" There was no response. "One, two, maybe more and counting."

"What do you want me to say? I told you what I know."

"I'm disappointed in you, David. Here I'm about to tell you how much you remind me of who I imagined my father would be like had he lived and you treat me like some asshole public servant."

Detective Turner's words reached me. Still, I didn't budge.

"David, you're in over your head. Whoever is behind this isn't going to stop until he gets what he wants. You could be his next victim."

I retrieved Turner's raincoat. "Drop in anytime, Russ if you're in the neighborhood or get lost on your way home to Maspeth, Queens," I said, as Turner put on his coat.

Turner placed a card in my jacket pocket and found his way out. Once he was gone, I went into the bathroom, turned on the shower and let the cold water drain the heat out of my skull. I dripped my way into the kitchen, had a glass of water. Not feeling a whole lot better, I decided not to take any of the pills Aldo gave me. In my state of mind, I didn't believe any pill would be potent enough to send me anywhere except straight to Hell.

XVIII. BLINDFOLDED

Why did I test Ilse when my life hung in the balance? Was it that I had to find out once and for all who she was with or was I trying to prove my trust in the woman I loved was greater than my father's for the woman he loved?

Another e-mail from Berlin: While your mother is a student at the University, she writes articles on the dangers of National Socialism. She interviews some of the victims of street brutality. The articles are timely and moving. The papers sell. Naturally, the publisher is pleased until one day he calls Freda into his office and tells her to tone down her pieces. She asks why. Instead of a good reason, he offers platitudes and vague generalities. Suffice to say there are influential people who feel Freda sees the issues from one perspective—the wrong one.

Thyssen, Krupp and other industrialists are men whose purpose is to build bigger and better cannons. They even sell them to Germany's enemies—if they can get their price. (Great Britain is a satisfied customer of Krupp during the First World War) The publisher says there is no proof the swaggering brown-shirted battalions victimizing Jews are anything more than a temporary phase. Freda refuses to retract a word and is sent packing.

Losing her job comes at the worst time. She's pregnant. I print the Nazi point of view for Otto Dietrich for a pittance. The inflation is at its peak. Winter looms. I'm going mad!

For my sanity, I play chess at the Romanische Café. Freda sits by the window. Kessler, who hasn't been in lately, arrives in a jovial mood carrying a paper bag filled with bananas. I tell him to be quiet or leave. Kessler puts his fingers to his lips, takes out a banana, peels it and hands it to one of the men watching the match. He repeats the maneuver until the bananas are gone. I see them being eaten and feel nauseated. A song plays in my head. It's a popular song being played on crystal sets in the neighborhood, "Yes, we have no bananas, we have no bananas today…" No one refuses Kessler's comic offering, while I try to keep from gagging.

Meanwhile, Freda stares out at the street. Kessler sees her face, takes out crayons a sketchpad and draws her in a wistful pose. When he's through he tears off the page and gives it to her. She smiles bravely. He sees the dark circles under her eyes, asks her to come outside where she can get a breath of fresh air. As if mesmerized, she follows. I'm so engrossed in my game I barely pay attention. Later, when I ask, Freda says Kessler took her to a café, bought her lunch and waited patiently while she ate. When she finished eating she tells him she lost her job. Kessler, whose eyes undress Freda every time he looks at her, offers her a chance to earn money posing for him.

Freda asks if she can accept the offer. At first, I refuse. We argue. In the end I give in. What can I do? Hunger has a way of limiting a man's choices. I warn Kessler not to take advantage of the arrangement. Kessler says he has no intention of taking advantage, having enough to worry about. He realizes I'm not so much of a Nazi as I pretend.

Another day, a blustery autumn afternoon. Kessler, collar of his trench-coat raised, ducks into the Romanische Café, makes his way through the smoke and lively conversations to the room where I'm about to play a game with a man wearing evening clothes. Perhaps, in these unpredictable, wasteful times, he's not had any sleep. He wants to wager a million marks. I think to myself: What good are a million marks? Tomorrow, it won't buy a loaf of bread.

"I'll play you blindfolded for your scarf," I say.

"It's made of silk."

"Will it keep the snow off my neck?"

"What do I get if I win?" the man asks.

"You can tell all your friends you beat the *wunderkind,* himself," Kessler remarks.

The man has obviously heard of me and accepts. Kessler calls the moves and offers his red handkerchief, with which he covers my eyes.

As a courtesy I allow my opponent to open. White moves King's Pawn to e4. I counter with Black King's Pawn to e4. The two Pawns face one another in the center of the board. White's second move is King's Bishop Pawn to f4, also known as the King's gambit. I counter by not accepting the 'free' offer to take a Pawn. Instead, I move my King's Bishop Pawn to f6. After multiple moves and countermoves, valuable pieces are whittled down. My opponent takes a Bishop with a Rook. I sacrifice a Pawn. My opponent brings up a Knight, opening his left flank. I keep my Queen under wraps until, like a heavy cruiser breaking through thick fog, she attacks. My opponent tries to elude the trap, but in his haste leaves his King unprotected, thereby sealing its fate. When I remove the blindfold, the man won't even shake my hand. He drops his scarf, leaves like a whipped dog.

Kessler helps me put away the pieces. On our way out of the

café I inhale the aroma of coffee and cake, hear my stomach growl and say, "What happened to the others?" Kessler, following closely, jokes: "Maybe, they're too hungry to get out of bed." Seeing me scowl, Kessler asks, "How's Freda? Is she well?"

"Morning sickness."

"Kessler doesn't respond. Instead he says, "I'd like you to meet someone."

"I can't," I reply, taking off at a brisk pace, my new silk scarf trailing in the breeze.

"Don't be in such a hurry," Kessler calls, catching up. "What does Dietrich pay you?"

I don't answer. Kessler, whose paintings have begun to sell, sees me in all my romantic futility, wanting to show Freda what noble sacrifices well up inside me whenever I think of her. "You're not fooling me. You're not like Dietrich."

"I'm still a member of the Party."

"What does Freda say about that?"

"Never mind what she says. Freda may pose for you, but I'm still her husband."

"Then, act like a husband."

"Who is this man?"

"We're almost there," Kessler says breathlessly, "You won't be sorry." We stop at the corner. "Only a little further…"

I'm not sure I want to do this. I don't like Kessler nor do I trust him.

"Why did you play the game blindfolded?"

"For the scarf. Maybe, I can use it the next time I play blindfolded."

"Maybe, you think a blindfold will keep you from seeing what's happening." I look at Kessler. "Don't you want a better life for Freda and your future son?" Kessler jabs.

I look at Kessler as if he's something vile. Kessler shrinks into his shabby coat. "I'm not a bad person."

"Where is this savior of yours?" I ask, testily.

Kessler points to a boarded-up building down the street. He leads me into an alley where there is access to what appears to be a deserted warehouse. Empty boxes are piled one on top of the other and packing crates litter the gloomy space. I can barely make out the figure of a man seated in front of a table. The man's fine tailored suit and topcoat, his neatly trimmed goatee, seem out of place in this dank hole.

"I've brought him," Kessler purrs.

The man looks at me with cold blue eyes. "Do you know who I am?" he asks.

"You're Emil Koenig, the foreign minister."

Kessler says, "What did I tell you?"

"What's your name?"

"Ernst Mannheim."

"Anton says you work for Otto Dietrich."

"I print a newspaper."

"Der Angriff?" I nod. "Do you write any of the filth you print?"

"I change a word or two now and then."

"I appreciate your candor, not your politics."

"Germany is in a bad way."

"Germany will be in a worse way if Otto Dietrich and his masters run things."

"I'm sure he says the same about you."

"I'm not interested in what Herr Dietrich has to say, only in what you have to say."

"Why choose me?"

"Because young men like you will be needed if Germany is to survive." He looks at me, at my torn jacket and solemn eyes.

"Anton tells me you have a wife with a child on the way." I nod. "I've heard your Leader's speeches. They make me sick."

Many nights Freda and I argue about the Fuehrer. She makes it quite clear as to how she feels. It makes me take a closer look at my own beliefs. If I really think Hitler and the Brown Shirts can save Germany.

Koenig puts his briefcase on the table. "I need someone to deliver the contents to the Interior Minister of Bavaria. We have enough evidence to stop these men before they can strong arm their way into power. The man who completes this mission will be a hero to the German people. I will personally reward him handsomely. Well, what do you say?"

I glare at Kessler for putting me in this position. I know if I don't do what's asked, Kessler will use it against me, won't stop until he gets what he really wants—Freda. "How do I know you'll keep your part of the bargain?"

"There's a safety deposit box at a bank. Inside the box is a bar of gold. You will be able to feed your family and outlive these terrible times. If you agree I can supply you with the name of the bank, a key, and further instructions."

"Can I give you my answer tomorrow?"

"Tomorrow may be too late."

"Why is that?"

"These men are planning to seize control of the government in Munich."

I look at the faces of Emil Koenig and Kessler and decide.

"When I return home I tell Freda what I intend to do. She cries. I cry too...until she agrees. We kiss and hug until I leave. I don't want to leave, but I must. It's the only way I can save my family from starving to death.

Inside the briefcase I find a ticket for a train going to Munich. It's crowded, but once we clear the city I find a seat. When the train stops in Augsburg, I get off to stretch my legs, see men wearing brown shirts in the direction I'm headed. I grip the briefcase tightly, look back over my left shoulder. Men wearing brown shirts come towards me. Something's gone wrong. How do they know? Have I been set up? Instinct tells me to run while I still have a chance. I tuck the briefcase under my arm and hurdle the narrow space between cars. On the other side of the tracks I light out in the direction of the town.

The men follow, but I get a good lead on them. I look back—see them struggle to keep pace. I put enough distance between us to give me a chance of finding a place to hide.

The houses look the same. A woman hangs wet clothes on a string line behind her house. I don't dare ask for help. She'll wonder what I'm doing on her street at this time of day. I get to the end of the street and turn the corner. There's a bakery. I'm tempted to go in, but decide on caution. There is an unoccupied building. I go in, find the stairs to the basement. I sit with my back against the wall waiting until it gets dark.

Climbing the stairs I think how much better my chances will be now that it's dark. I reach for the doorknob leading to the street and am blinded by a flashlight shining in my eyes. "We've been looking for you all over town, haven't we Dieter?" Dieter doesn't say anything. He's more interested in his blackjack. These men are different. They wear black shirts not brown and have a habit of asking questions to which they know the answers. I show them my party card. "I'm one of you," I say, in a friendly tone. "Your card is for a district in Berlin. What are you doing so far from home?" The man with the flashlight asks. Pointing to my briefcase, I say: "I'm delivering this to the Interior Minister." The man shines his light on his wristwatch, says, "You won't catch him—unless he sleeps at his desk." Like the others the smirk on Dieter's face comes naturally.

"Some men were chasing me," I say.

"I know. I'm one of them. So is Dieter. There are more of us outside," he says, grabbing my arm. I pull away. Dieter raises his arm. Then, the lights go out.

I won't bore you with details of what happens over the next few days. I learn Emil Koenig has been assassinated. They make it seem as if I've been duped by Koenig, Kessler and Freda. All Jews who see things differently. I don't agree with them, but they have a way of making you see things their way. So begins my basement indoctrination, in a cell within a cell, with the latest torture devices and guards who work in shifts.

They keep me awake around the clock trying to get me to incriminate Freda. One day, Bruno Schneider comes in with Otto Dietrich, my old boss from Berlin. I know what Schneider wants. I've played too many games of chess with him not to know. He wants Freda. Dietrich tries to get them to release me; Schneider is against it. For the time being, I stay put.

If Ilse wants you to go away with her she may be trying in her own way to persuade you to give up vengeance for something better. Ask yourself as I have, if following a road that offers no reward beyond the satisfaction of someday seeing swine punished is worth losing your chance for a life with the one you love.

I wrote back: You go to a lot of trouble trying to convince me your intentions are just and honorable. Save your family, protect your wife and unborn child, protect your grown up son. Words and endless justifications won't suffice. I don't believe your aim is to punish Nazis for their sins against humanity. More believable is, Greenberg showed you a way to redeem yourself and, like a drowning man thrashing around in water over his head, you grabbed it with both hands.

Restless, I finally went to bed, was soon awakened by a strange dream. In the dream I found myself sleeping with many people—men, women—all crowded into one bed. Some were being pushed out of the bed. Rather than sleep on the floor, they climbed back into the bed and tried to hide underneath those still asleep. When I tried to get into the bed I was told by a man in a black suit that only purebred Jews could crawl back in. I hid in a corner of the room and held my head as if a pipe had burst inside it. The deluge brought many bits and pieces of information to the surface—the most enduring one about how my mother managed to stay afloat against the rising tide of Nazi power.

I got out of bed, still terrorized by my dream in ways I didn't understand. I drank some water, wrote an e-mail to my father. Your stories of 'Little Walter,' Greenberg and Devorah are touching. I'm sorry I never flew to Berlin unannounced. Would you have been there—at 015 Kurfürstendamm or would your staff have prevented our meeting? I sent the e-mail and was surprised when I soon received a reply, forgetting for the moment that there was a six hour difference in time. It was 7 AM in Berlin; my father was awake.

Reply: I'll answer your questions as soon as I finish eating breakfast.

While waiting, like a schoolboy, I rested my head on the desk. It was a short nap, but long enough to produce yet another dream about the two women I loved most, neither of whom, if the truth were told, I knew very well. In the dream they bathed together in a marble bathtub and, without drying their bodies, joined hands in blissful nakedness as they walked, leaving behind them a trail of wet footprints.

I staggered down the hallway to the bathroom, threw back the shower curtain, turned on the shower. When I was through, I toweled myself dry. For some reason I felt more open to Ilse's point of view. What was to be gained taking care of old business when new business was at hand? Perhaps, the smell of perfumed soap and chlorinated water dazed me. Words rattled inside my brain. If only life was that simple, choose a path and follow it. Don't be lured by the promise of hidden treasure, nor seek a life of tracking an elusive past, putting off joyful moments for a struggle to the death.

My eyes picked up a grimy puddle left by Detective Turner's dripping raincoat. Seeds from our gritty conversation the previous night had begun to sprout. What might grow if I could connect events preceding the death of my mother to the day she died? I chewed on the idea until I didn't like the taste. At last, I checked my e-mail and found my father's frantic message.

Has something happened, David? Have they come for you? For God sakes, please answer. Damn this infernal machine with its open-ended invitation to run off at the mouth. I wouldn't be surprised if it puts people like me out of business someday. Hear that, David? I'm worried about you. Don't you know how much? Even if you're so used to my words coming from another source, I'm that source.

After alerting my father that I was all right, I received a message back. "Sorry for my attack on machines. Thank God for laptops and beds that put you in a position to tap out messages like a woodpecker. Try not to misunderstand. Does a father have the right to expect his son to respect him no matter what he's done?

Does he have the right to expect his son to feel his pain if that son chooses to focus solely on the pain he's caused others? What compels me to write is I've begun to understand how close we are—separate yet closely bound by synchronous thoughts. I believe what it's done, without our knowing, is set our hearts to solving the same confusing puzzle. I finished my coffee, poured another cup, took a sip and returned to my father's words.

I stayed with Devorah when I returned to Berlin. There's an advantage in living a long time despite the everyday struggle of getting out of bed, seeing a face you don't recognize in the mirror. You pick up a bit after breakfast, have more resolve to make the day—perhaps your last—count. There's another dreary afternoon ahead of you, a nap after lunch, a drink before dinner, a book and shuffling feet into the bedroom.

Sometimes, your eyes won't close. And, things, what your life once was, come back in jabs of gratitude, sprints of bygone passion that eddy in a river filled with water so clear you can almost see the bottom. Yes, and fountains of belief. Time passes. You ask yourself: Belief in what—certainly not in the future? You breathe a few times and when you're satisfied it isn't your last breath you close your eyes. I do my best to follow Devorah's suggestions— swallow vitamins, eat a nutritious diet. I even pray. The spiritual aspect of life, one I sorely neglected, I must admit has some meaning for me.

At last it comes! I will tell you the story of how your mother, how Freda lured men out of their dull and insipid lethargies. If this was her intent the matter might easily be put to rest. But, what if, as it seemed to me, she had no ulterior motive, but merely lived inside a guarded castle with the pure and simple belief she would be allowed passage to the land of her dreams in the arms of her rescuer and one true love?

David, can you imagine my excitement when Freda tells me she's pregnant. It's a day I will never forget. Not only am I hungry, I'm happy. It's hard being both so I play chess and try to concentrate on the board. Every so often I glance over at her, those wistful eyes, such ineffable longing. She looks away. Where? It's then I see the affect she has on others—who don't only show up to watch me cut the swine to ribbons. In their eyes they believe she will be open to their amorous advances. Each time she looks away they feel it. Do you know where they feel it, David? In their penises. Among the model citizens sitting on their erections are none other than Anton Kessler and Bruno Schneider.

The Gestapo knows the story. Whether they got it from Kessler or Bruno Schneider or from someone else I can't say. When they force me off the train in Augsburg, it's not hard for me to figure out I've made a terrible mistake. The torture I endure over the following weeks is easier to take than the evidence with which they pound down my resistance. I'm shown photographs of Freda with other men, intimate letters she writes, signs sworn statements of witnesses telling what they see and hear. Pregnant or not, it sounds as though she is part of a demimonde.

I wonder why they don't shoot me and have done with it. In time their reasons become clear. They feel my ability playing chess shows a keen mind that implicitly understands strategy in terms of 'men' and how they can be best utilized. For nine years they keep me locked in a room in the cellar of a house in Augsburg. Every so often, they bring me out of my dungeon to teach men they feel will someday be leading soldiers into battle. I teach chess strategy under tight security, with little chance for escape. Still, I try. Each time I'm caught and beaten for my troubles by men that enjoy their work. Eventually, I lose my desire to escape or get word to anyone, though I never stop thinking about whom your mother might be sleeping with. Naturally, they continue to add fuel to the fire raging inside me by telling me they are protecting me from doing to Freda what they are doing to me.

At his trial in March of 1924, Hitler is sent to prison for his part in the 1923 Munich putsch. He uses the time to write *Mein Kampf* (*My Struggle*) and plan the Party's next move. Upon his release, he takes up where he left off. He personally pays me a visit in my 'basement hotel' and impresses upon me the importance of these training sessions. To set the chessmen in place for what's to come. One day, not far in the future, chessmen take the form of U-boats, Messerschmidts, Tiger tanks and V-rockets.

When Adolf Hitler is named chancellor, a wild celebration loosens the tongues of my guards. I overhear them talking about someone I hadn't heard of in years, Anton Kessler. Before I can ask them anything, they and others like them are transferred to posts where their experience as guards no doubt can be better utilized. David, has it occurred to you that there might be one thing that keeps us apart—your mother?

I wrote: Do you blame her for what happened to you?

My father wrote back: I know she posed for Kessler, but I've never seen any of those paintings, David, have you?

I thought it strange for him to ask me that. Still, no matter what he said it wouldn't change my plans. In fact, his words made me more determined to find out what paintings decorated the walls of Carl Schneider's Fifth Avenue apartment.

XIX: Daughters of the SS

Perhaps, I didn't make it clear to my father as to what I was after. Yes, revenge, but also evidence of a painting I had long imagined. One that pointed a finger.

On the day my mother appeared, not an angel with wings, but dressed like a prostitute, she seemed surprised when I told her I'd spent most of my life trying to find the people responsible for her death. When I wanted to know more she said I needed to find the answers on my own. This brief encounter continued to annoy me. It was Saturday morning; I wasn't in the mood to answer questions from either one of them.

As I left the building a woman carrying a bulky satchel came towards me. She was about to pass me by only to stop and say, "Pardon me, are you David Menard?"

"I am."

"Rosalie Gehringer, Mr. Sunshine's secretary," she said, her reddish hair shining in the early light. "We spoke on the phone. Do you mind if I walk with you?"

"How did you know where to find me?"

"When you called you left your name. The rest wasn't hard."

"Have you heard from Marty?"

She shook her head and bit her lip, for the moment unable to speak. "I'm sorry to hear that," I said, walking on. "There's a diner around the corner. Would you care to join me for breakfast?"

My eyes fell on the satchel she carried. "Let me give you a hand."

"I brought you a present. I'll show it to you after breakfast," she said, holding the satchel close to her.

The place was almost empty. After glancing at the menu, we ordered. There wasn't a long wait for our food. We ate as if we were breaking a fast. I was almost through eating when my curiosity got the best of me. "Tell me, Miss Gehringer, what brings you out so early?"

"Don't you know?" she said, assuming I knew something. It gave me pause. Hadn't I done the same thing by assuming my father knew what I was after, my mother, too? She lifted the satchel onto the table, took out a leather-bound picture album. I recognized it at once. It was the job I did for Marty before he went to 'Nam. "Marty wanted you to have it," she said.

"Did he say why?" The woman shook her head. "I would think a person like you would appreciate it, as a memento."

"There are too many bad memories in it for me."

"Were you born in Germany?" She nodded.

"So was I. I was nine when I left."

"I was there during the war. I came to the States in 1955."

"I'd never guess. You speak English flawlessly."

"I've worked hard at it."

"Germans always work hard."

"I knew plenty who were shiftless bums."

"So much for generalities. Is there something you must do, Miss Gehringer?"

"My friends call me, Rosalie."

"Nice name...Rosalie."

"Marty said you were thinking about taking down some dangerous people. If they're who I think they are I'd be making plans to get away, far away."

I signaled the waitress for more coffee. "May I have a look?"

Rosalie turned the album around. I went through it page by page. It wasn't until I came to the last few pages that I began to see photographs with which I was not familiar. The pictures weren't like the ones of the peaceful German countryside or of a small church wedding in hard times or were they part of Leopold Brennermann's "Dachau Collection." These were taken at a camp where officers and doctors relaxed. The close proximity of the spa-like camp to the death camp made the photographs extraordinary since they corroborated accounts of the matter-of-fact approach the SS took toward the people they were disposing of and brought to mind a letter I received in which my father used the image of men dancing on the graves of its victims.

One photo was of a man sitting in a comfortable chair reading a magazine. For some reason it had a powerful effect on me. I looked at it closely until it hit me—his eyeglasses. They were the same ones I'd seen in a portrait of Ilse's father, gold spectacles of large magnification. Though younger in this photo, it was Stefan Van Ness. He had the sleepy-satisfied expression of a man who'd been treated to more than a bit of relaxation provided by two *Fräuleins,* one sitting on the floor next to him, the other with her head resting in his lap.

There were others I didn't recognize, either by name or reputation. One was of a man who signed his name: "With love and kisses, Bruno." Something told me it was Bruno Schneider. He, too, like Dr. Van Ness, was in a state of utter bliss. "They look like they were having a good time," I said, laconically.

"It does, doesn't it?"

"What is it, Rosalie? What's bothering you?"

"Not all the men at the camps were officers and gentlemen."

"Do you mean the average SS?"

"To the German people the SS were considered above average."

"Didn't they do some of the killing?"

"I've read they sloshed around ankle-deep in blood all day."

"Do you believe that?"

"Anything's possible."

"Then, they knew."

"What?"

"That they were taking part in the systematic cleansing of a race of people."

"You give them more credit than they deserve."

"What should I do, exonerate them for being stupid?" Rosalie sighed, her breasts rising in her chest like dough in an oven.

"Were you close to that sort of thing?" I asked.

"I worked for Mr. Sunshine for over thirty years. We discussed many things that required the utmost confidentiality."

"If you're asking me if I'd offer the same confidentiality, my answer would be, 'yes.'"

"Marty thought highly of you, Mr. Menard or I wouldn't be here."

"Call me, David."

"David...I think his judgment, at least in this case, was correct."

"You flatter me."

"I hope you won't be shocked by what I'm going to tell you." Rosalie bit her lip and said: "I lived in the same house with an SS."

"Not a boyfriend."

"No, not a boyfriend. He was my father. We lived in the same house, but I seldom saw him. He left for work early, came home late. My sister and brother were in *Gymnasium* and didn't mind not having a father telling them what to do. I was a little girl. I wanted my father to read me a story, tuck me into bed, kiss me goodnight."

"I see," I said seriously, drawn in by Rosalie's story.

"Do you? Can you imagine what a child remembers? One night my mother was in the kitchen preparing something for him to eat when he came in. They didn't say much to each other until they closed the door and went to bed. I could hear them arguing about something and forced myself to stay awake."

At that point in the conversation the waitress came to the table with the check. After she left, my eyes encouraged Rosalie to continue. The momentary break in her story gave her time to think. "Perhaps, I shouldn't be telling you this," she said.

"Why not?"

"It could get me into trouble."

"What kind of trouble?"

"Did you forget Marty?"

"I haven't forgotten. Can we go back to the night you stayed up late?"

Seeing how much it meant to me she continued. "I heard my father go into the bathroom. It sounded as if he was washing his hands. When he finished he went back to their bedroom. Before he closed the door I heard my mother crying. Then, I fell asleep."

"Sometimes, I watched her wash his clothes. The black shirts, pants, socks, even his underwear. Once when I was seven or eight she saw me looking, and before I could turn away, she said, "Why are you looking at me that way, Rosalie?"

"I didn't know what to say. Finally, I said, "You rub so hard it

182

makes your hands red, mama." She began to cry. I went over to her, hugged her and told her not to cry, but she couldn't stop. Doing what he did—perhaps, 'sloshing around all day in blood'— blood must have crept into every crevice of his skin, into every pore. It was as if he could never remove the smell of the slaughterhouse from his person. I could only imagine what it was like for my mother sleeping beside this man when he crept into bed."

When I asked if I could keep several photographs, Rosalie said, "You can have the entire album with my compliments."

Outside on the sidewalk, she said, "I made copies of the important photos. They're in a safety deposit box. Should anything happen to me, I've arranged to have them sent to people I trust. They will know what to do with them."

"One more thing, after the war was over, the only way I could accept my father was at a distance. If I kept him out of my mind, away from anything or anyone I valued, then I could go on ringing him up on the telephone, doing due diligence as his lone surviving child. Whenever he showed up in the flesh I was mortified, though I did my best to keep it to myself, making it barely tolerable. I was, after all, trained to be strong. The daughter of an SS."

With that she stuck out her hand. I took the firm handshake with a firm handshake of my own. I wasn't sure what to say. It seemed too soon to say goodbye. Rosalie sensed my uncertainty.

"Your plans don't coincide with mine or I might offer to make you a real German dinner some night." I didn't answer. "I wish you luck," she said, crossing the street, waving goodbye.

I watched her walk away holding the empty satchel, put the photograph album under my arm and began walking. I walked to Broadway, noticing the drivers, how they avoided slamming into each other. Their uncanny avoidance of one another seemed the greatest proof of our instinct to survive. Life moved fast in the city—sometimes sweet, sometimes sour, but never without the element of danger.

xx. CAREFULLY SELECTED PHOTOGRAPHS

reached Ilse's place early and rang. I was surprised by the sound of Ilse's footsteps coming down the stairs. "You're early," she said, opening the door, leaning her head over to kiss me lightly on the lips.

"I had to see you."

"Here I am," she said, twirling like a girl, her accordion-pleated skirt billowing to show off her legs.

"How did you know I'd be early?"

"Because I know you."

"Ilse, tell me something."

"Can I tell you anything?" she asked.

"Say whatever your heart desires."

"Sounds nice. Still, you don't mean a word of it, do you? Tell me my darling, do you know many Germans?"

"I've known a few. Shall we walk?"

"Let's walk and talk or shall we talk and walk," she said, as if she'd been drinking. I took her arm, steadied her. "I've known quite a few Germans," she said, more soberly. "They fancy they can hide anything about themselves and get away with it. How well do you know Carl?"

"I've heard a few things come out of his mouth that caught me by surprise."

"Had he been drinking?" I nodded. "He loosens up when he drinks. The day he married my sister, we were drinking champagne. I don't recall when he switched to whiskey, only that he came over and asked me to dance with him. He was stinking drunk and I tried to get out of it, but his arm hooked me around the waist and pulled me close. While we danced he asked me if I approved of him as a brother-in-law. I wasn't sure what to say, so I thanked him for his many kindnesses since my father's death."

"What was his reaction?"

"He became quiet. Finally, he said, 'Trudi is a fine woman. She will be a good mother someday. But, I don't love her in the way you might think.'"

"Then, why did you marry her?" I asked.

"To spare you and Trudi further suffering."

"How can we be spared when our mother is locked up in a mental hospital?"

"She will soon be back to normal," he said, "the doctors are confident they can bring her around."

"What's wrong with her?"

"She blames herself for your father's death," he said.

"Why?"

"It's those *verfluchte Juden*. They murdered your father."

"Have you notified the authorities?"

"Never mind that. We'll take care of the ones responsible our own way."

"Why does Mother blame herself?"

"After the war she pleaded with your father to leave Germany. But, when they arrived in Argentina she became homesick."

"She was always so happy," I said.

"One reason I married Trudi is to prove how devoted I am not only to your sister but to you and your mother. Be careful, if anything happens to Trudi I might come looking for you." Then, he laughed, as if it was a big joke.

"I told him I was flattered by his offer, but made it clear he should never speak to me about this matter again. He smiled, not in the least bit worried. He knew I wouldn't tell Trudi on her wedding night or any other night. How could I?"

"Does Trudi see this?"

"Trudi doesn't see or say much. She's had several miscarriages. No more turns at bat for big sister. Meanwhile, Gisele bears Carl two sons."

"Where do the children live?"

"They're in a private boarding school."

"Military?"

"You could call it that. They'll be home any day now."

What about Trudi?"

"She accepts the boys as if they are her own children. It's truly remarkable."

"And, the boys, how do they feel?"

"They believe she's their mother."

"What about Gisele?"

"As long as Carl pays attention to her, buys her things, she's fine."

"What happens when she doesn't get what she wants?"

"Carl is patient with her, but strict."

"Isn't he afraid she'll talk?"

"She won't talk. Do you want to know why?" I nodded. "Because every so often Carl shows her carefully selected photographs of the good old days."

The wind had picked up. I could see Ilse was upset. I hailed a taxi, gave the driver the address. We got in, neither of us speaking for several minutes. Finally, Ilse turned towards me. I stared straight ahead. "You look tired," she said.

"Do I?"

"You probably didn't get much sleep."

I faced her. Her eyes were red. I wasn't sure if it was from lack of sleep, too much alcohol, from being upset or a combination of all three. I leaned towards her. She pulled back. She said, "I've been thinking about my mother. David, I'm afraid for her."

"Have you heard anything?"

"No, it's just a feeling I have. All these years they say they can't get through to her, that she doesn't communicate with anyone."

"Doesn't she keep in touch with you and Trudi?"

"The only letters I receive from Argentina come from her doctor." I remembered the texture of the envelope, how alike it felt to my father's. The man who wrote it had trouble with English.

"Perhaps, the shock of seeing her husband murdered..."

"David, she's not crazy," Ilse interrupted, "Don't ask me how I know. I just do."

I was about to reveal what my father said, but stopped short of providing Ilse with information that might further compromise my own position, uncertain enough to think Ilse might question the source of my information.

The driver pulled to the curb. I paid him, got out first and then helped Ilse out. When the cabdriver drove off, Ilse looked at me differently. She brought her body close to mine. I took her in my arms, felt her hot tears on my cheek and said rather obliquely, "We'll be okay if the ammo holds out." Her tears turned to laughter, as two men with high-pitched voices, identical crewcuts and leather jackets ran by, battling a wind that seemed intent on blowing them off their course.

I held Ilse to keep her upright. "Is that a line from a cowboy movie?" she asked, shivering.

"Every cowboy movie."

"You're funny."

My eyes wandered upwards. Someone observing us ducked into a fistful of drapes. "You're cold," I said, "Let's get inside."

As we climbed the steps to the front door, Ilse said: "Take me to the movies sometime, David."

"New movie or old movie?"

"Old movie—from your time."

I smiled. As I opened the door, she said: "Sweet David."

In the vestibule she pressed the intercom button, gave me a little squeeze. Louis' voice came out garbled. "Ilse," she said loudly into the tiny microphone. The buzzer sounded. Once inside, in a moment of weakness, the fear I'd die without anyone knowing anything about who I was or what I'd done, made me stop short. Before Ilse could say anything, I asked, "Are you with me?"

"Don't you know how I feel about you?"

In the elevator I had another thought. "Will we have the pleasure of Bruno Schneider's company tonight?"

We got off the elevator on the third floor, walked down the hallway toward Carl's apartment. "I don't know," Ilse said.

I tried to read Ilse's mind and wondered when the time came would she be on my side or against me. At the door, Ilse said, "Be careful, my love." As I leaned toward her, I said, "Is he well?" She nodded, pulled back the instant the door opened. Louis, serious as always, eyes averted, showed us inside.

Approaching the living room, I heard Carl's voice barreling

our way. When he saw us, he stopped in mid-sentence, got up from the sofa drink in hand. Trudi, looking attractive in a black and white linen suit, white shell earrings and black pumps, sat legs crossed in a high-backed chair.

Carl took a sip of his drink and said, "Come in, come in." He kissed Ilse on the cheek, pointed me to a seat on the sofa. Ilse wandered over to a chair to be near her sister.

"So, tell me, David what goes on in the world today?"

"Just the usual raping and pillaging."

Ignoring my attempt at humor, Carl impassively finished his drink and asked, "Can I get you something, Ilse?"

"Whatever you're having."

"Champagne, of course. What about you, Mr. *Buchbinder?*"

"Champagne in honor of the artist," I said, adding, "of course."

"Tonight we celebrate Trudi's great success. *"Nicht wahr, liebchen?"* Again, Carl lapsed into a language he felt comfortable with despite growing up in Argentina, living most of his adult life in the United States. I thought the lapses were intentional, designed to make him sound foreign-born and therefore not responsible for his carelessness with a 'second' language.

"Naturally, I'm elated. Who wouldn't be? The show will bring in old people and new money. That's what you mean, Carl darling, isn't it?"

Carl finished his champagne and motioned to Louis, who refilled his glass. "How many times must I tell you? Serve our guests first." He smiled. Louis nodded and returned with two glasses of champagne on a tray. He served Ilse, then me. "That's better," Carl said, putting an exclamation point in the middle of Louis' shoulder blades.

"What was I saying? No, Trudi. I'm a slave-driver, isn't that right my dear?"

"If you insist."

"I chain her to the easel."

"He makes the word 'easel' sound like *'Esel.'* What means *'Esel' auf Deutsch?"*

"Doesn't it mean 'ass?'" I said, innocently.

Carl's face turned red. "More champagne," he called, as soon as he finished his glass. Louis came to the rescue. He poured quickly; Carl pulled back too soon. A few drops fell onto the white carpet. "I'm very sorry, Herr Schneider," Louis said, bowing.

"Never mind, Louis," Louis clicked his heels and backed out of the room. Louis pronounced Carl's name correctly, Schneider not Snyder. For that, I was grateful.

"I propose a toast," Carl said, getting to his feet, "To the success of art," lifting his glass, "And, to great artists." He looked toward Trudi and raised his glass higher.

In doing so, more champagne spilled from his glass. Trudi got up and Carl said, "Leave it!" Trudi paid him no mind, went to the hall closet. She brought back an old towel and wiped up the damage.

"Now she's satisfied," Carl said, "With some women it's very easy. Would you agree, David?" Carl looked at Ilse, then at David and said, "Don't pay any attention to me. I'm having a good time." By now the level of his voice had reached a higher pitch, his face almost purple. "Trudi is very good at creating harmony out of chaos."

"Sounds like a desirable talent," I offered.

"One I'm afraid I don't possess," Ilse chimed in.

"Nor I," Carl said, finishing his champagne. Louis entered with the bottle and carefully poured. "Much better, Louis," Carl said, turning to me, "Isn't that what you do, David, tie up loose ends?"

"I suppose it is."

"Don't be so wishy-washy. Someone might take you for one of the 'chosen people.' You're a *Buchbinder,* aren't you?"

"May I ask for what are they chosen?" I said, finishing my glass and signaling for another.

"I don't know. I left Germany when I was a baby."

"I was nine."

"*Nein,*" Carl joked, "What *ja?*" When no one laughed at his pun, he said, "Such a dull crowd. Okay, David, tell us when did you leave the Fatherland?"

"1933...And, you?"

"1945."

"Once the war was over."

"My father got a job in Buenos Aires. That's where I met my beautiful bride. *Nicht wahr, liebchen?*"

Looking at her wristwatch, Trudi said sourly, "I don't want to spoil your fun, Carl, but shouldn't we be on our way?"

"Why don't you and Ilse grab a cab? I'd like to chat with David, maybe smoke a cigar. Louis will drive us over when we're through with our conversation."

Louis stood to attention at Carl's suggestion, hearing it as a command.

"Come, Ilse, we let the men have their cigars in peace," Trudi said, getting to her feet. "And, get some peace of our own."

"I don't mind the smell of cigars," Ilse said, "My father smoked them. I'd walk alongside him trying to keep up with his long stride to catch the smoke in my nostrils."

"You always were a daddy's girl. Don't tell me I have to go to my showing alone?" Trudi said, pretending to be superfluous in this new configuration. "It will be such an embarrassment I won't be able to show my face ever again."

"Don't stay on my account, Ilse," I said. "I'd like a moment or two with Carl myself."

Ilse did her best to conceal her disappointment. "As you wish," she said, finishing her champagne and putting the empty glass on the mantel. She took her sister's arm and said, "I won't desert you, Trudi."

"Good girls," Carl replied, a streak of chauvinism running down his back. Louis accompanied the ladies to the door, helped them on with their wraps and let them out like well-trained schnauzers. Carl went to the bar and poured himself schnapps. When he was through pouring, he looked over at me and asked, "Will you join me?"

"By all means."

This pleased Carl. As he poured there was an unsteadiness I hoped would become more pronounced. I drank slowly so as not to rush what seemed ready to spill from our host...counting on my tolerance for alcohol to keep me on top of things.

Handing me my drink, Carl said, "May I be frank?"

"I see no reason for friends to stand on ceremony."

"I want you to know how much I admired you from the start."

"That's nice of you to say."

"I mean it. There are so few from the old days who take life the right way, who are able to see what interesting events may be in front of us."

"Are you referring to anything in particular?"

"Who can predict the future?" Carl drank deeply and for a moment let the liquor work its magic. "The only fault I find with you is this obsession you have for Anton Kessler."

"I admire his work. What's wrong with that?"

"He was a traitor to his people. The main thrust of his work was obscene—caricatures of a starving population, grotesque portraits of the most abject, pitiful excuses of humanity." Carl's words contradicted his auction speech that in retrospect seemed to be done solely for the benefit of prospective buyers.

I was careful not to mention Trudi's copying Kessler's work, the money Carl made from the sale of those copies. Instead I said, "I won't argue those points. They were extremely difficult times and, after all, painters like everyone else have to eat. I believe Kessler did other paintings, some of which were considered among his best. If any are still around, they may prove quite valuable."

"Valuable? Nonsense! Yes, well, maybe to a certain extent."

"I don't wish to be rude," I said, finishing my drink, adding, "Especially since I'm drinking your cognac."

Carl went to the bar, brought over the bottle. "Speak freely. We're not children," he said, slugging down what was left in his own glass, pouring another.

Knowing Carl had photos of my letters, but not wanting to broach the subject I chose my words carefully. "Kessler's work, as told to me by my Uncle Kurt, especially sketches he made of my mother, is highly regarded by experts in the field."

"Your Uncle Kurt said this?"

"In letters he sent to me," I said, playing dumb.

"When were those letters sent?"

"I received the first one in the Sixties."

"I find this quite remarkable since your 'Uncle Kurt' died in the *Wehrmacht's* noble retreat from Stalingrad—some twenty years before."

"How do you know that?"

"We know people who were there."

"They must have him mixed up with someone else."

Carl snorted. "Don't you know who you've been correspon-ding with all these years?"

"Not my Uncle Kurt?"

"How are you at absorbing shocks?"

"Terrible."

"You have a strange sense of humor, my friend."

"No stranger than yours."

"Do you really think we have something in common?"

"What about the 'printer picnics'?"

"The picnics were held before either of us was born."

"But, not before our fathers were born."

"The night we went out for beer you said your father was dead."

"Both fathers!"

"Is it possible you were wrong about one?"

"Which one?"

"Don't be a smart-ass. I'm not amused." I became silent as a stone. "The fact is your father, to our best knowledge, is alive." Carl walked to his desk, removed a key from his pocket, opened a drawer, and pulled out a folder. He read from it as he walked around the room until he stood somewhere behind me. "Ernst Mannheim worked for the Party from 1923 until the end of the war in 1945. He dropped out of sight, but resurfaced in Berlin where he worked in construction while attending the university. He graduated in 1964 with a degree in Medicine. He did post-graduate work and later opened his own practice as a psychiatrist."

"He's probably dead by now. If he were still alive he'd be a hundred years old," I said, emboldened by my belief that Carl hadn't seen our more recent correspondence.

"I think you know where he is. I warn you, you'd better have the right answers."

"You're barking up the wrong tree, my friend."

With that and before I could turn around, Carl came up behind me and boxed one of my ears with his fist, followed it with a hard slap across my face before I could cover up. Even as blood trickled from one nostril, I didn't retaliate.

"You mongrel-Jews are all the same. Cowards! You think because your Christian-born father was useful to our Fuehrer it makes you impervious. Your mother was a Jewish slut." I tightened my jaw. "Go on, take a poke at me," Carl snarled. I controlled my anger. Carl continued. "You will soon find out how impervious you are, how easily we break you."

"Is that because of Louis?"

"Louis, *kommensiemitt,*" Carl said, lapsing into German.

Louis came into the living room and stood at attention. "Soften him up, Louis."

While putting on a pair of pigskin gloves, Louis looked at me, shook his head. "What's wrong?" Carl asked.

"If I hit him I might kill him."

"One less mongrel-Jew...the Fuehrer himself would pin a medal on your chest."

"Herr Carl, I don't think Herr Bruno would like it if something should happen to him before he arrives."

"You're not paid to think. I'm in charge."

Louis looked at his wristwatch. "It's seven-thirty. Herr Bruno's plane will land in less than an hour."

"Maybe, you're right," Carl said, taking an uncomfortable step backwards. "My father is fussy. He doesn't like bloodstains on his expensive carpet. You'd better get started, Louis, if you're picking him up. Meanwhile, I'll keep our guest entertained."

Louis did an about face and left. As I reached into my pocket for a handkerchief, Carl, standing behind his desk, took a gun from the drawer—a Luger. "Too bad about your nose," Carl said, prodding me to my feet. "Shall we see what interests you so much you poke that nose of yours where it doesn't belong?"

As he pushed me down the hallway, Carl continued his rant. "Do you know what my biggest regret is? I never see those precocious nephews and nieces of yours with their new fountain pens and durable canvas book-bags and monkey-like eagerness to please; or your aunts and uncles with their thick glasses and short-sightedness. Your grandparents with their soft arms, poor digestion and mincing ways when they take their showers. Then, of course there was your mother, responsible for bringing one more mongrel-Jew into existence. Open the door," he ordered, adding, "Too bad we didn't get to her sooner."

What did he mean—get to her sooner? Was his demented logic that the world would be spared a 'Mongrel-Jew' or did the Nazis have the opportunity to kill her before I was born, but for some reason chose not to?

Carl pushed me into the room, snapped on the light. There was a painting on the wall over the bed. It was of a middle-aged woman whose overwrought condition was revealed in prominent veins on the back of her hands, hair pulled back in a chignon, and by a disbelieving face shown in pinched distress and puffy-eyed disillusionment.

"I can tell you're not pleased," Carl jabbed, "Too bad. I thought you'd like something different for a change."

At this point, I knew that whatever I said would have incensed Carl all the more. If I didn't say anything it might be taken as disrespect and push Carl further over the edge.

"Who's the artist?"

"Who do you think?"

"Trudi?" Carl nodded. "The woman looks like she's lost everything she values."

"That's because she has. I can see you're curious. Don't you recognize Ilse's mother, Sabine?"

"We've never met."

"Of course you've never met. She's been in a mental hospital until recently when her heart gave out."

"Does Ilse know her mother's dead?"

"Trudi will tell her. Trudi is a wife who understands her place in the New World Order." Carl waved me out of the bedroom with his Luger. As he reached for the switch to turn the light off, I thrust the weight of my shoulder into him, the force of the collision knocking the Luger out of his hand. Carl absorbed the blow by bracing his back against the doorjamb. In the split second I had to decide whether to scramble after the gun or use my own weapon, Carl brought his knee up into my groin, doubling me over. He pushed me out of his way and went to retrieve the gun. Recovering my balance, I chased Carl down, kicked the gun away just as he was about to pounce on it.

Carl used his weight advantage to push me aside and went after the Luger as it slid along the parquet floor, coming to rest at the entry. I was tempted to settle matters with my own gun, but chose not to risk letting Carl get his hands on the slippery Luger. We were scuffling on the floor when the door flew open.

The blurry image of a man I met at the cocktail party, who had introduced himself as 'Alex Berg,' came into focus. Behind him, Louis had drawn his gun. The man's reaction to two grown men fighting like children was almost paternal, "What seems to be the trouble, boys?"

"He took my gun," Carl whined.

"Take better care of it," the man said, "Get up. I'll take care of Mr. Menard."

"How did you make out, *Vati?*" Carl asked, once he was on his feet.

"How do you think?" the man said, his face pink with the flush of victory.

"Do you believe this?" Carl said, to no one in particular. "He's 101 years old and continues to dominate in a sport for 80 and 90 year olds."

I thought, Of course! How stupid of me? The man wasn't Alex Berg. He was Bruno Schneider.

"My swimming was strong and effortless. My running needs improvement."

"He wants to improve," Carl said, mockingly. "Can you imagine a man his age?"

"That's enough, Carl. Go make a pot of coffee."

My eyes flirted with the gun lying a few feet away "Louis, make us some sandwiches. I'm starving. The kind I like only lighter with the mustard," Bruno Schneider said, taking a Walther automatic from his coat pocket and training it on me.

"*Hände Hoch!*" he said. I raised my arms. Waving the gun, Schneider motioned me toward a room down the hall. When Carl followed, his father said, "Pick up your gun and get me a drink, the usual, *schnell!*"

Carl retrieved his Luger and headed for the bar. I was ordered to open a door midway down the hall. Once we entered the room, Bruno Schneider jammed his gun into his pocket, said, "You can lower your hands, Mr. Menard. You must think me blind not to see what your intentions were."

My father was right about Bruno Schneider. He was nobody's fool. "You seem agitated, Mr. Menard. It will go easier for you if you tell us what you know. Surely a man of your age would be wise not to get involved in something of this nature."

The room had the antiseptic feel of a doctor's office. There was an examining table on the far wall flanked by a glass cabinet on one side, by a sink and vanity on the other. Anatomical charts of the human body—muscles, bones, etc. covered the walls. The air had a pine scent; if one closed his eyes he might think he'd been transported to the Black Forest.

Schneider motioned me into a large walk-in closet. He snapped on a light. "Have you ever been in a hyperbaric chamber?" I shook my head. "Well, you're in the latest version of one now," he said, adding, "It's amazing the effect it has on injuries to the human anatomy. For example your bloody nose and red ear show signs of marked improvement."

"What about you, Herr Schneider?"

"Most men my age have trouble getting out of bed in the morning."

"Do you sleep in a closet?"

"I don't need to. I feel at the top of my game."

"What game is that?"

"Never mind the chit-chat. I warn you. There's only so much I can do before Carl gets his hands on you. Carl is a good boy, not like the mad dogs portrayed in your movies about the fanatical exploits of the German military. Still, Carl feels a sense of pride standing up for what he knows is right. The Germany I knew as a child is no more. It was a good Germany in some ways. In other ways it reminds me of what this country seems headed towards—inflation, unemployment, dissatisfied people. The Fuehrer changed all of that for Germany, at least for a while. You think we lost the war? Let me remind you wars are never won as long as there are men like Carl and Louis ready and willing to fight."

As Schneider changed, he began to laugh for what reason I had no idea. I only knew his course laughter angered me. In a way

I was grateful. It made the words come easier. "Your beloved Fuehrer took poison rather than face the tribunal, caused misery and suffering for millions, his own people included. That can't be erased—not in any future war you imagine to be on the horizon. To those like you who say he brought better times to Germany, I say at what cost? I was only a boy when his deranged ideas..." With that, Bruno Schneider came out in his underwear and slapped me across the face with the program from "Tristan and Isolde."

It was my turn to laugh as I stood there in amazement as this tautly muscled centenarian looked at me with such fiery hatred I thought he'd burst into flames. Strangely enough my edginess was gone, as though the slap or the laughter brought me to my senses. That and the amazing air in the makeshift space gave me a second wind. Meanwhile, Bruno Schneider finished dressing without another word spoken. With great self-control I chose to wait, hoping they wouldn't realize at some point that I was armed.

Bruno Schneider motioned me to back out of the closet. He wore a pale green hooded robe that gave his skin the look of an old, Italian monk. He had on tinted eyeglasses of a kind I'd never seen before. Moments later, Louis entered holding a large tray with triangular sandwiches of pumpernickel and slices of the finest imported cheeses and deli meats. China cups were filled with olives, pickles and sauerkraut.

Bruno Schneider ate lustily, waved for me to join him. I shook my head. Carl came in, handed his father a glass of dark beer. There was something about the way he chewed that attested to his vitality. That and the fact he seemed to be in constant motion.

When he was through eating, he opened a cabinet and selected several bottles from an array. Louis poured water into a cup from a glass pitcher. Schneider swallowed several capsules with the water, scooped the powders into what remained of the liquid, stirred it with a spoon and drank the mixture slowly, in equally spaced intervals. No one spoke until he was through. Carl, who appeared sober, said, "Let me have him, *Vati.*"

"You nearly lost him. I have him now and I assure you I won't lose him."

"*Vati, bitte.*"

Bruno Schneider shook his head decisively. "Louis, be so kind as to inform me when the women return." He turned towards his son. "Carl, why aren't you with your wife? It doesn't look good for Trudi to have to deal with those kikes without support."

"Ilse is with her."

"Since when does Ilse own the gallery?"

"I thought I could do more good here."

"Have some coffee and put ice on your face. It looks as if you ran into a bowl of tomato sauce."

Louis broke into a smile, which dissolved as soon as Carl threw him a stern look. He removed the empty dishes and left the room, followed by Carl. Bruno Schneider took note of my demeanor before addressing me again. "So tell me, Mr. Menard, what brings you to our side of town?"

"I was invited for cocktails."

"Tell me the real reason."

"I came to find out things about my family."

"Did Carl tell you that I knew your father?"

"He said that you and he played chess as boys."

"He was the best chess player in Berlin before he was twenty. People came to watch him...sometimes to test their skill against his."

"How did they do?"

Bruno Schneider smiled sardonically. "Not as well as they anticipated. Mr. Menard, tell me are you in touch with your father?"

"My father died before I was born."

"Are you certain of that?"

"I was told he went on a mission and never returned."

"We know otherwise."

"What makes you say that?"

"Never mind that. Who do you think wrote letters to you? And, who more than likely is still in touch?"

"Do you mean the letters I received from my Uncle Kurt?"

"Your Uncle Kurt died in the snow at Stalingrad."

"I know you have a copy of our correspondence. Isn't that proof enough?"

With the blood rising in his face, Bruno Schneider shouted, "It isn't proof when we know it's a lie."

"I don't know what to say."

"Start by telling the truth."

"First, tell me why my mother was tortured?"

"What makes you think I have any knowledge of that?"

My declaration was made without great expectation, more in the realm of using an aggressive move to keep my opponent off balance. What surprised me was the response.

"If I tell you what you want to know, would you then tell me what you found or were given by one of your partners?"

"I have no partners."

"Not anymore. Mr. Kyle Charlton and Leo's son Martin will no longer be meddling into affairs that are none of their business."

"I went to the gallery hoping to buy a Kessler. I'm still interested."

"In due time. We think it's possible you may have stumbled onto something."

"What?"

"How is it you haven't mentioned your friend?"

"Aldo?"

"Was that his name? Too bad he had to die for nothing. I wonder why you haven't said a word about our taking film from this so-called friend of yours."

"Do you mean how he was murdered in cold blood?"

"Any ideas as to who might be responsible?"

"I thought it might be Carl or Louis."

"What about me?" I shook my head. "You think it's not possible?"

"I think it would be difficult."

"I'm not saying I did it, but why not me? I am in possession of all my faculties."

"Yes, except for one. My guess is macular degeneration of the retina, with limited central vision. You saw me look at the gun on the floor out of the corner of your eye."

"You seem to know a great deal about this condition. Is it possible you have a similar condition yourself?"

"I see well enough without glasses."

"As an old friend of the family, can't we do business?"

"Sorry, I'm not in the market for old furnaces."

"Of course, you know about that from your 'Uncle Kurt.'"

I nodded.

"Anyone who connects me to those times is kaput," Bruno Schneider said, reaching into his pocket, pointing his gun at me.

"If you kill me I assure you that you won't find what you are looking for."

Bruno Schneider licked his lips. "Tell me exactly what it is you want?"

"How did Freda Mannheim die?"

"Why don't I begin with what I know about Leopold Brennermann, the adjutant at Dachau, a very astute man? For one thing, he knew his camera. What he didn't know was how the pictures he took came out. I had the film developed and am satisfied that none of the photographs he took of me showed my face. Yes, we know about his diary. He smuggled the evidence out of Dachau, thence out of Germany to the United States, I assume, that upon his death, he left it to his son's care. Mr. Sunshine, as he was called, passed the diary and roll of film on to Mr. Kyle Charlton, which you found in his beach-house. Correct me if I am wrong."

"How do you know what I found?"

"You had company on that trip, didn't you?"

"Ilse?"

"Correct again. Didn't you suspect something?"

"No," I said, trying to keep my emotions from weakening my position.

"Carl thought you might have additional information you'd be willing to share with us. For once he was right. "

"I haven't told you anything."

"You didn't have to."

Bruno Schneider's countermove gave him the advantage. I let him think he'd outsmarted me. I knew what he wanted. He wanted the man who beat him at chess.

"There may be something else I might be willing to share."

"Yes, much better, Mr. Menard. You'll see that once you get to know us we're not so bad."

I remember the words to a song that had the melody of "Yes, We Have No Bananas" from the first Nazis—not soldiers, but Gestapo—who came to my school when I was nine. I realized I had to do something to gain the upper hand.

"Where is the portrait Kessler did of my mother?" I asked, hoping for a miracle.

"Are you quite sure we're talking about the same Kessler?"

"I won't know until I see the one you have, will I?"

"And, for this prize what can we expect from you in return?"

"What about the black book?" Schneider shook his head. "Perhaps, an additional photo..."

"I don't believe you," Schneider broke in.

"Show me the portrait and you can accompany me to my apartment. If you don't like what you see you can kill me the way you ordered the others killed."

"Patience, Mr. Menard. We're not interested in killing you just yet. Do you know why I don't believe you? It's because taking pictures in those days was a much more difficult task. In the confusion, I'm surprised Leo was able to get any clear shots. I think you're trying to protect your father, the man who unceremoniously left you on the doorstep of strangers in a country completely unknown to you, who didn't possess a fatherly instinct, but instead falsified his identity using his brother's name instead of his own to his son and at present leaves you at our mercy. Until you tell me where he's hiding, which is a matter of some importance, since he's part of a group responsible for tracking down some of our best people, we keep you alive."

"I believe Leo took enough shots to provide a reason for plastic surgery. With one photograph in my side pocket, I can afford to wait," I said, "Just as you feel about the photograph I say exists and my father, who I say doesn't, I feel there's a painting you keep around for whatever reason I would like to see with my own eyes."

"You use the English language cunningly for someone born in the Fatherland," Bruno Schneider said, waving me forward with his Walther—through the hyperbaric chamber. As we were coming out into the bedroom I glimpsed several women's wigs in open boxes. Most had white or gray hair and could have been used as a disguise by someone handy with make-up or having a background in the theatre.

With the touch of a button Schneider illuminated the room from lights recessed in the ceiling. I looked around, was surprised at the contrast of heavy, antique furniture—an armoire, a chest of drawers, two marble-topped tables—as you might see at an old Victorian inn or museum contrasted with more contemporary pieces ...stainless steel, new fabric for curtains and floor, electronics of the latest and best design, partial to German expertise—naturally.

At a control panel by the side of his bed, Schneider flipped a switch and the wall over the bed separated. A painting set on a track trundled forward. I felt like a nervous schoolboy about to give a recitation, with one major difference. My mother wasn't in the audience. She'd been immortalized on canvas, her mutilated body resembling the way she looked in the alley—bloodied from many wounds. Kessler painted in a way that even her nakedness could not disconcert. It was lewd and provocative, conceived as only a twisted, demonic mind could.

My eyes were taken to a place they'd never been before. I could do no more about my disgust than I could walk on my hands. It brought a smile to Bruno Schneider's thin lips, but made me croak: "It's the work of a madman."

"What about the object of his desire?"

I looked at Bruno Schneider and wondered who was more responsible: Kessler, the man who committed the barbarous act or the man standing in front of me.

"One question," I said at last, "Did Kessler do this alone or did the Gestapo have a hand in it as well?"

"She was in bad shape when I found her," Schneider answered, ignoring my question.

"When was that?"

"About the same time Kessler was sent to Auschwitz."

I knew there was no way that could be true. She was dead by then. "Are you saying you found the portrait after the Gestapo had their way?" I saw the look in Bruno Schneider's eyes, how mesmerized he was, how he was unable to take his eyes off her.

"Don't you see what he did to her?" Schneider said.

"Did Kessler do this himself or did he copy what he saw?"

"The Gestapo questioned her and let her go."

"On whose authority?"

"On my authority."

I leveled my gaze at the charred bottom of the frame. "Someone tried to burn it."

"I only treated her wounds."

I saw where incisions were made in the canvas. How crudely they'd been 'stanched' and 'bandaged' with paint. "You were in love with her, weren't you?"

"Everyone was in love with Freda Adler," Bruno Schneider said, rubbing his hands together, adding: "At night when we're alone she comes alive. Naturally, I come alive too."

"Not in your wildest dreams."

"Don't you see what I've done? I've softened the bruises, wiped away the blood." He was trying to convince me of his profound love for her as expressed in the role of demented caretaker. It didn't work, I wouldn't let it. "And, cut."

"There was no other choice. I did it in order to save her."

The man was a raving maniac. I had to push him harder. "It's obvious these surgeries were performed without the approval of the artist."

"I take full responsibility."

"Only Kessler has full responsibility."

"What you see now is not the original."

"Of course it isn't. It's a miserable, second-rate collaboration with someone who doesn't know the first thing about art."

"If that's how you feel," Schneider said, taken aback by my callousness. "There's more at stake here than art. But, what does it matter? The name was burned beyond recognition."

I took a closer look and said, "A blind man can see Kessler's signature at the bottom."

At last, a tortured expression broke out on Bruno Schneider's taut face. He began to wheeze.

"Perhaps, it wasn't Kessler," I needled, "Perhaps, the great Furnace-maker himself, the man who came up with the idea and the machinery to kill more Jews in less time, tried to destroy the evidence."

"That was a long time ago," Bruno Schneider said, controlling his cough, holding his position by pointing his gun. It was then I realized the Walther was solid gold, a one of a kind model that could only have been given him by the Fuehrer himself. He had it pointed at my heart.

I didn't flinch, kept talking. "Maybe, it was," I said, "you're still taking liberties. Your actions mirror the cancer doctor who sits at the wheel of a car in darkness, not sure where he's headed, how he'll get there or if he'll get there."

"I don't see myself in that light."

"Perhaps, you need a stronger pair of eyeglasses. You're too concerned with removing parts of your victim's anatomy: A cyst in the ovaries, a nodule in the thyroid, a mass in the chest, a tumor in the brain. The worse the disease is, the more grim the terminology. Whatever you think doesn't belong you remove, you murdering swine."

"What are you babbling about? I'm not a cancer doctor. You have the wrong man."

"Tell me, Herr Bruno, who is the right man?"

"I see what you're up to you clever little monkey. You put me alongside cancer doctors. It isn't about them it's about Freda Adler, your beloved mother." He continued calling her by her maiden name Adler, not her married name, Mannheim. "There are two men who could have done this," he said, "One of them was Kessler. If you look closely you can see how deep his feelings went. Examine the way he painted her eyes. How it must have torn him up inside seeing her looking at him day after day, accusing him."

"Who was the other man, Herr Bruno, was it you?"

"She was never mine. But, a jealous husband might take revenge on the woman who betrayed him."

"Do you expect me to believe that?"

"From 1924–1933, Ernst Mannheim played chess in no formal competition. In fact, there is no record of him anywhere."

"More likely he was solving military problems for the Third Reich. It may have been the price he had to pay for staying alive, for keeping my mother alive. What makes you so interested in him you'd go back that far?"

"You said you believed he was dead."

"You've convinced me otherwise. If a man sends letters and

signs them 'Uncle Kurt,' wouldn't you believe him? I'm willing to admit I was wrong, but I'm not convinced my father played a part in her death."

"What else are you suddenly willing to not be convinced of?"

I realized speaking too openly might get me killed, especially if I pressed him on the question of guilt. I wondered, what if with Hitler as the new chancellor, Kessler knowing his days were numbered, gave the painting to my mother? When she was arrested by the Gestapo on charges of being part of the underground, she gave up Kessler. But, when the Gestapo believe she's been lying to save her own skin, they torture her. What if Bruno Schneider convinced the Gestapo to give her to him on his own recognizance? Yes, he drove her home, consoled her. What if in looking for bandages, he found Kessler's work and went mad?

"Well, what is your answer?"

"Forgive me. My mind wanders. Tell me, what must I do? Will you sell it to me?"

"You don't have that kind of money."

"What if I can put you in touch with the ones you seek?"

I saw the look in Bruno Schneider's eyes. It was the megalomaniacal glint of a man incapable of accepting anything less than his own way. I wondered, how do I reach a man who can't hear a word I'm saying?

XXI. THE WOLF'S LAIR

I could hear their voices. Trudi and Ilse had returned from the gallery. With his Luger looking like an unwanted appendage, Carl planted a kiss on his wife's cheek.

"What in God's name is going on?" she asked.

Bruno Schneider pressed the barrel of his automatic into my spine and whispered huskily: "Walk in front of me as if nothing's wrong." I did what I was told, except I walked down the hallway faster than the old man expected. He kept pace. When we were close enough, seeing blood on my face, Ilse said, "He's hurt."

"He's fine. Isn't that right, Mr. Menard?" Schneider said, slipping the automatic into the pocket of his robe.

"He's right, Ilse. I'm fine."

Carl and Trudi joined us. Schneider said, "Keep Mr. Menard entertained while I lie down." Carl smiled as if he'd just received a field promotion. "Have Louis wake me in an hour," Bruno Schneider said, before retiring. Carl told Louis to put his gun away and take up his post at the entry.

"Did you have some kind of disagreement?" Ilse asked.

"It's not your concern, Ilse," Carl said.

"There's blood all over your shirt, David. Let me help you clean it."

"The shirt looks better with some color," Carl taunted, following us into the bathroom. Trudi came too.

"Carl, leave them alone. I want a word with you," Trudi said, adding, "Put that thing away."

Carl, caught in the crosshairs of two angry women, relented. He put the Luger into his jacket pocket. "I can't believe you never showed up. I was mortified," Trudi said, "The Frankmans kept asking 'when is Carl coming, when is Carl coming?' What could I say? What could I do?"

"What displeased them? There wasn't anything to their liking?"

"I was too busy fending off questions about you to be myself. Good thing Ilse was there."

"Why is that, *liebchen?*"

"Carl, do me a favor. Your jacket's filthy. You look like you've been in the sack with someone."

"Only with you, *liebchen.*"

"Why, has Gisele gone back to mama again?"

"Don't be so smart."

"I'll be anything I want."

Carl took off his jacket, looked at the woman he'd controlled without so much as a peep—until now. She took his jacket, gave it to Ilse to hold while she shooed Carl down the hall like a mother hen. "Put on something comfortable, Carl. That nice smoking jacket I got for your birthday would be perfect."

"Perfect for what?"

"I'm not sure I'll ever forgive you for what you did to me tonight," Trudi pouted. "If it wasn't for Ilse we would have lost a lot of money."

"What did she do, a striptease?" Carl said, as he went to change.

"Carl, do you realize how crude you are sometimes?" Trudi called, as I followed Ilse out of the bathroom.

I'd taken several blows to the head, but wasn't badly hurt. Ilse's open show of affection helped my morale. We went into the living room. Trudi found her chair. Ilse sat beside me on the sofa. Trudi said, "The old man will be up soon." Before she could say another word, Carl came into the room wearing a red, yellow and black smoking jacket.

"What do you think?" he asked Ilse, who replied, "You look like someone wrapped you in the German flag."

"What a nice thing to say."

"It wasn't meant to be nice."

"We were just having some fun, a little roughhouse."

"Don't you think you're too old for such things?"

"Never too old for anything."

Ilse looked at me and said, "Trudi, read our mother's letter, will you, the one she wrote to you before she died?"

"What letter? She was never given permission to correspond..." Carl said angrily, his voice trailing off once he realized he'd said too much.

"So that's why we never received mail from her. I should have known."

"Surely, you don't believe that I had anything to do with it. I was merely following her doctor's orders."

"Who gave him the orders?" Ilse asked. "It was you, wasn't it?"

"I did what her doctors told me to do. If they were responsible I will make sure..."

"Come on Carl," Ilse broke in, "You've been calling the shots all along."

"That's not true, Ilse. I put her in the best place for her kind of sickness. I made sure she had the best treatment. And, I paid the bills. For many years, I paid."

"You didn't pay enough." Ilse said, slipping her hand into the pocket of Carl's jacket, the one Trudi gave her. I had the feeling she'd found the steel Luger, that her slender fingers had molded to its unique shape.

"You killed our father," Ilse said, "Why?"

Carl started to chuckle. Ilse took out the gun, pointed it at him. Carl froze. "Now, you must pay for it with your life."

"Ilse, be sensible. Please, there is no reason to do this. I didn't give the order. My father did."

"Why?"

"He refused to do the operations."

"Don't you mean you couldn't bully him anymore?"

"I never meant harm should come…" Carl cried out, alerting Louis. "I never meant…" Ilse fired one shot into Carl's belly. Carl fell, clutching his stomach. As Louis came into the room, I drew my gun and fired. The bullet stopped Louis in his tracks. As he fell he got off a wild shot. It caught Ilse in the chest. The gun fell from her hand as she sank to the floor. Seeing Ilse, Trudi broke down, tearfully knelt beside her sister. Louis was dead. I kept an eye on Carl, writhing in pain on the floor crying for his mother. Then, I also knelt. Ilse opened her eyes when I touched her forehead. "I'm sorry," she whispered.

"Trudi, call 911!"

"Anyone ever tell you…?"

"Take it easy." Ilse nodded, closed her eyes as though the pain was too great. She pressed her hand against her chest. Seeing her hand smeared with blood, I said: "Help's on the way."

Ilse opened her eyes. "Anyone ever…" Again, she couldn't finish.

"You…Only you."

Trudi returned and said, "I called. Can you imagine, they said they were too busy, that I should call back later?"

"What?" I looked at Trudi with disbelieving eyes. When I looked down at Ilse, she lay still. I knew. She was gone. Trudi made a terrible sound. I slowly got to my feet.

I thought of Bruno Schneider, whether he'd heard the shots. I wasn't sure if Carl had any fight left in him, how much I had myself. I took a calculated risk. I picked up Carl's Luger, handed it to Trudi. Giving her the responsibility of keeping an eye on a husband who had deceived her in every possible way brought her back to reality.

I gripped my gun, edged my way down the hallway. I passed Bruno Schneider's door, heard nothing and waited for him to make the next move. Not the best approach in chess where advantage generally went to the offensive-minded player. But, unlike my father, I'd never learned the rigid orthodoxy of the chess masters.

I positioned myself along the wall near the kitchen and waited. It wasn't long before the door opened and a shoeless Bruno Schneider tiptoed into the hallway. He looked both ways, but didn't see me pancaked against the wall behind him.

A shot was fired. It came from the direction of the living room. "Carl is that you?" Schneider called, advancing cautiously. *"Was ist los?"*

Getting no answer, he tiptoed closer. I silently followed. Reaching the living room, he raised his gun to fire. As he did, I crept up behind him, placed my gun in the small of Schneider's back and said stiffly, *"Hände Hoch!"* Schneider hesitated.

"What's this all about, Mr. Menard? Are you trying to trick me with a pen or is it a pencil?"

"Does this feel like a pencil?" I said, jamming my gun into Schneider's ribs.

The Nazi jumped. "Drop it—now!" I ordered. Bruno Schneider obeyed. I picked up the automatic, pushed Schneider into the living room. Trudi still held the Luger I'd given her. Bruno Schneider sank into a chair, covered his face with his hands.

"I could never bear to see an animal suffer," Trudi said.

I saw the lifeless body of the woman I loved. Darkness had crept over her...deep and impenetrable. To shock me back to my senses, Trudi said: "David, I'm going to wash my hands. Keep an eye on Herr Bruno." There was blood everywhere. I nodded.

Once Trudi was gone I saw a change in Bruno Schneider. I recalled my father's story about the Nazi in the hospital in Buenos Aires, the one who killed his good friend.

Suddenly, Schneider raised his head and out poured the slime, "I must tell you something. The ones in the camps—we did them a favor. I can't tell you how many of them came to me and pleaded to be put to death. Some wanted to save their children. They offered their lives as payment. I'm telling you they didn't want to live. They were tired of living because they knew how poisonous they were to everyone they came in contact with in German society. They didn't like themselves. They were in fact anti-Semitic. Can you believe it? It's true. We were doing them a favor. Please, believe me I'm no monster. I'm a man just like any other man. I once had a family. My children, six in all except for Carl, were killed in the war, some from bombing raids, several in combat. My wife Ola died of a drug overdose in Argentina. I've known suffering. Still, I'm alive.

"Before the war, we'd sit down to supper together. We told stories, drank beer, laughed and cracked jokes. We had good times. We didn't try to hurt one another. We were good to be with. We liked people. Do you think I wanted to do this terrible thing? I was forced to do it. They forced me."

"Who forced you?"

"You know who. They did the same thing to your father. We never had a chance."

"Who could force you to invent such a terrible device?"

"*'Wolfchen'*...Do you know who I'm talking about? Of course you know. You were only a boy, but you do remember demonstrations, parades, the sound of the drums, soldiers marching in the streets, raising their legs in unison. He said the Third Reich would rule the world for centuries to come. We were The Master Race—stronger, smarter able to follow orders and carry out our mission. *'Wolfchen'* was a name given him by an old matriarch whose ass he was kissing for her dough. He sat on the floor near her feet, while she stroked his head calling to him, *'Wolfchen...Mein wolfchen.'*

"I've had plastic surgery. So many surgeries, my wife didn't recognize me. I don't hate Jews. They're not so bad once you get to know them. They're just as good as the next guy. But, nobody is perfect." Schneider grew rhapsodic. "Carl wasn't around in the glory days. It's all right. His sons will carry the flag for him."

"They're Gisele's sons."

"The little bastards are learning the truth about history."

"Sounds like the little bastards are good little Nazis in training," I said, before injecting, "You won't be around to see it."

"Carl will see it," Schneider said, on the verge of losing his grip.

"Carl *ist tot,*" I reminded.

"Put Carl in front of an audience and he has them eating out of his hand. He organized neo-Nazi underground groups and activities in every state, won converts wherever he went."

"No doubt, he'll be missed."

"He'll be in the trenches with the others."

"How often do you speak to your grandsons?"

"Enough to know they'll be good soldiers someday. The thirteen-year-old and I play chess sometimes. He plays to win," Schneider said, "Sometimes he does win." Off on another tangent, he said, "Der Fuehrer took over the Fatherland when people were starving, cold and without work. He changed things and soon they will change again. Our determination will bring ultimate victory. We must work in secret for now. That too will change. I can go out in public because I was smart enough not to be photographed. If someone took my picture and I got my hands on him he was finished. No one has a snapshot of me from 1933–1945, and no one is left who can identify me."

"What about my father?"

"He hasn't seen me in fifty years. He wouldn't recognize me."

"And, this?" I asked, showing him one of the photographs Rosalie gave me. "This and others were taken at a rest camp for the overworked high-ranking officers of the SS and doctors like Stefan Van Ness."

Bruno Schneider reached for the photograph. I pulled back, offered it again. Before I could stop him he grabbed the picture and tore it to shreds.

"Don't you like the picture? I like it. I liked it so much I made a dozen copies and sent them to all my friends."

"Liar."

"Should I write their names and addresses down on a piece of paper for you?"

"I can take a joke as well as the next one. While you try to decide what to do with me, what about playing a friendly game of chess?"

"How do you know I play chess?"

"Your friend had a chess set in his apartment."

"It was you...you filthy, malignant swine," I said, losing sight of all reason. Seeing my words have no effect, I hit him with the butt of my gun. It tore a chunk out of his face.

"Bastard," he cried, stanching the blood with his fingers. "What's the matter, afraid to step out of your father's shadow?"

He was a tough old bird, not afraid to die.

"You should pay more attention to what I'm saying."

"Poor Herr Bruno. Are you so used to giving orders having men do what you tell them to do?"

"Some men need to be told. What's the matter, Mr. Menard?"

"Shooting you would be too easy."

"That's it, Mr. Menard. Half-Jew. Half-German. You have a tough choice. Go on, be a Jew, make it hard on yourself."

"Where's the board?"

"That's better. I will show you, the pieces are set up," he said cheerfully, as if the wound in his cheek was already beginning to heal.

Trudi came in holding a glass of mineral water. "What are you going to do with Herr Bruno?" She asked, saw his face and smiled. "Kill him, David, kill him."

"How come you didn't complain all these years, Trudi?" Schneider said, mildly.

"Because I didn't know there were men in the world as evil as you."

"Tell me Trudi, do you like being a respected artist?"

"You know I do. Who wouldn't?"

"Living on Fifth Avenue in New York City?" Trudi nodded. "You like being able to buy the finest clothes, go to the best restaurants, indulge yourself in whatever selfish whim or desire makes you feel good? There's a price to pay for it—for everything. Be patient, Trudi. The world is turning all the time. It will soon come back around to the good old days in Berlin."

"I don't know anything about Berlin or the good old days."

"There were a lot of people in Germany just like you. They didn't want to know. Still, they liked the champagne and caviar."

"I'm going to lie down," Trudi said, only to stop herself and say, "David, there's something that may help you understand how it was for Ilse. When our father died the world changed for us. I married Carl because he said he'd take good care of me and would do the same for my mother and Ilse. Not until yesterday when I received a letter written in my mother's own hand did I know the truth. On our way home tonight from the gallery I gave Ilse the letter to read. Ilse loved our father more than anyone until she met you. You put her in a difficult position, yet her thoughts were only of you. She wanted to protect you from harm. She said, 'I love David, Trudi. I love him more than words can say.'"

Bruno Schneider couldn't resist jabbing, "Such tenderness." I thanked Trudi for telling me, pushed Schneider forward. In the bedroom, Trudi asked, "The painting over your bed. Whose work is it?"

"Whose do you think?"

"Is it a Kessler?"

Bruno Schneider didn't answer. "Is it Freda?" Once more, Schneider was silent. "It's hideous, yet there's a quality that seems to be trying to force its way out. Too bad Kessler spoiled it."

"Jews spoil everything."

"Carl told me you were in love with this woman."

"Carl didn't know the full story."

Trudi looked again, "Yes, quite a woman."

"She was a slut. Kessler wasn't the only Jew she fucked."

I let his coarse remark pass like dirty water down the drain.

"Did you know Freda Adler was Mr. Menard's mother?" Schneider said, testing my resolve.

"I didn't."

"Perhaps, you also don't know my own relationship with her."

She'd gotten him talking. If I took a step back, perhaps he'd go further and admit what until now I could only surmise.

"I'm a lot different than Carl. I won't tolerate a woman laughing at me."

"I'd never do that to you." Trudi glanced towards me. I nodded—barely.

"What if you found a younger man, someone you couldn't get out of your pretty little head?" Schneider questioned, missing eye contact between Trudi and I.

"I'm more loyal than you think, Herr Bruno...especially if my needs are being met."

"Are you teasing me?" Schneider looked up at the painting. "She teased me."

Trudi laughed playfully. "Did you slap her around?"

"Take another look, my dear Trudi. Take a good look."

"You tortured her?"

Schneider laughed like a madman. "Don't you believe me?"

"Of course, I believe you, Herr Bruno. Why shouldn't I?" Trudi said, doing her best to hide her fright.

"Are we going to play chess or talk?" I said, pretending not to hear a word that was said.

"Excuse my rudeness. Let's begin, shall we? Since you're my guest I give you choice of color," Schneider said.

"I choose white," I said. When the board was in place, I moved my King's pawn to d4. I glanced at my watch. It was almost midnight. Trudi found herself a comfortable chair, but expressed no interest in the game. After an hour, Schneider took his concentration away from the board, said: "Trudi, ask Louis to make some sandwiches."

"Herr Bruno, Louis is indisposed."

"I know it's late. Wake him up."

Trudi could barely keep herself from laughing. "If I could wake the dead it wouldn't be Louis."

"I'm hungry," Schneider whined.

"He's hungry. You sound like the boys."

"When will they be home from school?"

"I've been expecting them to call. They were due in this afternoon. Once they get to the city they want to see everything, go everywhere. "

"Do you have enough food for the young lions?"

"Right now, I'm more concerned about how they'll take seeing their father lying dead on the living room rug."

"Be a good girl, Trudi," Schneider pleaded.

"I'm not a girl and you can no longer treat me as if I were your servant."

I stared at the board. "Shhh! Can't you see Mr. Menard is concentrating?" Schneider pointed toward the kitchen. Trudi got up from her chair and left the room.

"Can't we work something out, Mr. Menard?"

"I thought we were playing chess."

"We are. Trudi, do me a favor?"

"Trudi's gone and you get no more favors," I said, bluntly. "It's your move, Herr Bruno."

There was no mistaking the look on Bruno Schneider's face. It was clearly one of desperation, the man indirectly responsible for more deaths than any other man in the living world. There was something else, a factor I couldn't measure—what effect time and tempo would present a man of one hundred and one who'd competed in an athletic competition earlier that day. Bruno Schneider won the event, but at what cost? And, how much of his vitality did the infusion of vitamins, minerals, enzymes and oxygen from his private chamber, not to mention a catnap, replenish? They built the human body strong in the old days—Übermensch and other comic heroes. But, even the so-called 'Supermen' had their breaking points.

I remembered my brief interlude on the phone with a woman who insisted she was perfectly content to pass on what seemed to be a valuable Kessler to someone who resembled her older sister. Perhaps, Bruno Schneider used the wigs in his closet as part of a disguise for playing the role of older sister before eliminating the generous younger sister with a bullet neatly placed at her left temple or the maid who cleaned up the apartment at the Olympia Towers to get at Charlton, the woman I saw on the stairs to kill Aldo and, finally, someone who pretended she was Rosalie to get Marty Sunshine.

The wigs were of high quality, most likely human hair; the kind of hair that was in plentiful supply at Dachau, taken from Jews after they were gassed and before they were thrown into the ovens. Leave it to Bruno Schneider to collect human hair, maybe as far back as the day he played chess with my father dressed as a woman.

Trudi returned with a cell phone to her ear. "The boys are at Grand Central. They want Louis to pick them up."

"How much do they know?" I asked, while Schneider's eyes were still glued to the board.

"I told them about their father," Trudi whispered.

"What was their reaction?"

"I think they've begun to realize they were cursed from the day they were born."

"I believe it's your move, Mr. Menard," Schneider said.

"Take a taxi," Trudi said into the phone, adding, "I'll have something for you to eat." All at once she was beaming with pride. As she left, Bruno Schneider said, "Can I have...?" One look told him he wasn't in a position to receive anything. "If you don't treat me like a prisoner of war, I'll report you to the authorities."

"You were caught out of uniform behind enemy lines," I replied, moving my Knight to an advantageous position. "Geneva Rules are not in effect."

"Rommel would know how to counter your obvious attempts to secure favorable position."

"Why don't you give him a call?"

"If I felt I needed him, I would."

Bruno Schneider's lapses into unreality were a delight to the ear. I needed to push him harder, force him to the breaking point, as if anything could break the Furnace-maker.

"Haven't you heard, Herr Bruno, everyone needs someone?"

"You're a clever man, Mr. Menard. How do you Mongrel-Jews manage to be so clever after all we've done to you?"

"Practice."

Meanwhile, Bruno Schneider rambled, "Your attempt to lengthen the game won't change its ultimate result. See!" He took my brave Knight with his Bishop.

"Smirking won't help your cause."

"My cause, as you put it, is something you know nothing about." Rather than respond, I kept my attention on the board. I moved my Queen so she could attack from any direction, practically guaranteeing Herr Bruno would lose one valuable piece: his

Rook or the bloodthirsty Bishop. "You've made a mistake, Herr Bruno. You'd better call the *'Afrika Korps.'*"

"I don't need the *'Afrika Korps.'*"

Waiting for Bruno Schneider to make the next move, I thought of my father, his valiant efforts to capture a Queen every man coveted; what its effect had on him.

Bruno Schneider's Knight pawed at my Queen, but lacked the fury to capture it. I countered by moving my Kingside Rook one square to g1, giving more support to my Pawn at g4.

"What if I told you there were a thousand neo-Nazi groups armed and ready to receive my instructions?"

"It's your move, Herr Bruno."

"Didn't you hear what I said? Do you think I made that number up?"

"You're sweating, Herr Bruno."

My insolence infuriated Schneider. "I'll show you the names and addresses of our membership," he said, his upper lip quivering.

Bruno Schneider reached his left hand into a small drawer on his side of the table. Before I could react, his hand was inside. It came out with a second Walther pistol. My hands shot into the air.

"Lower your arms, Mr. Menard. At least until we finish the game."

Still, I wasn't done for—not yet! He was so intent...so sure his position on the board was secure that he failed to disarm me. His left hand that held the gun, steadied. But, with each succeeding move, the time it took to decide, his hand slowly began to drop.

It was my turn to lay siege. I stared at the board until it cracked open, until I entered the breach. As each of Herr Bruno's pieces fell one by one, I felt its effect. I was amazed that, at game's

end, he looked at me without rancor. "You're not who you pretend to be," he said. When I didn't respond, he added, "I should
have known. You're Ernst Mannheim's son, though I pity the
both of you."

"Has something happened to my father?"

"I was referring to your similar talent for chess. It's clear you
and your father cannot rise to the challenges of life."

As though to show me he meant business, he raised his gun. I
thought, he'd most likely circle around behind me to shoot me
in the left temple. As he rose from his chair, he came away from
the table so I couldn't interfere with his design. I waited until I
heard his breathing, felt his exhalations make the hair on my neck
stand on end. My gun was under my belt. I inched my hand
closer to it until I made contact, then slowed my breathing so as
not to alert him. I could smell the odor of sweat from his armpit
as he raised his pistol. In that split second, I withdrew my gun,
and, while sliding off my chair, I fired.

He took the bullet in the left shoulder, his pistol dropping to
the floor. I stooped down, picked it up and put it into my coat
pocket. While he lay there bleeding, I went into his bedroom,
felt the presence of my mother in all her obscene nakedness. I
tried to see into those battered eyes. The thought of what terrible
things they'd done to her filled me with an uncontrollable rage.

I turned back toward the chess room, spotted a book of
matches on the nightstand next to Bruno Schneider's bed. Herr
Bruno didn't appear to be a man who read books by candlelight,
not with so many expensive light fixtures in the room.

I opened the drawer. There sat a box of cigars. Not ordinary
cigars, but Cubans, the same brand as the ones at Kyle Charlton's
beach-house. Herr Bruno got around. I thought of Aldo...the old
lady who passed me on the stairs. I thought of Rosalie, her father.

I got a little crazy. It was like hearing my father describe how he felt when he visited Dachau.

I took the book of matches and struck one, put the flame underneath the painting. It began to smoke. I had to strike several more before the canvas caught fire. Once the smoke curled toward the ceiling, I realized the whole place could go up, that the evidence of what happened might be destroyed.

I went into the bathroom, took several large towels, put them in the sink, soaked them with water and returned to the bedroom. Somehow, Bruno Schneider had mustered enough strength to get to his feet. He stood next to the panel of buttons by his bed. He pressed one, bringing the painting forward until it fell from the track onto the bed.

The canvas had caught fire in several places and was spreading quickly. Herr Bruno threw his body over the canvas, trying to smother the flames. His clothes caught fire. When the flames burnt his skin, he screamed a sound I'd heard many times before in my dreams. I threw the soaked towels at him and headed for the hallway. I'd almost reached the front door when I was overcome by smoke.

I sometimes thought of Bruno Schneider as a wild bird, his sharp beak of a nose, his collection of female feathers; his half-closed eyes in the midst of blind orgasmic ecstasy. He was finally dead, yet I still felt the blackness of his soul press heavily on my chest as I drifted in and out. Floating in the ethers of an air-zone you reached without postage due. People stood around, watching, waiting. An alarm sounded. They quickly assembled for a fire drill. I tried to tell them not to worry, but no words came to my lips.

When I awoke I was in a bed at Mt. Sinai Hospital with tubes in my arms and an oxygen mask over my face. A nurse checked my vitals. There were many faces in the room. When the mask was removed, some of the faces had names.

"What happened?" Detective Turner asked.

"I was about to ask you the same question," I said, groggily, "Did the place burn down?"

"A Mrs. Trudi Snyder called the Fire Department. We found four dead bodies in the apartment. Only one died from smoke inhalation."

"Bruno Schneider."

"According to a credit card we found, his name was Alex Berg."

"It's not his real name."

"Trudi Snyder thinks you're a hero."

"She say why?"

"I was hoping you'd fill me in."

After they got some solid food into me I told Turner the story. On the day I was discharged, Turner called to tell me there'd be an inquest. I'd have to appear. I told him it could be dangerous to my health. He said he'd provide surveillance until everything was straightened out.

Had I known what was in store, I might have run away with Ilse. That was if I had my father's gift for running. What was I looking for? Marty Sunshine said sons follow a predetermined path begun by their fathers. If he was right, how many generations of Mannheim men worked so hard for so little?

The first thing I did when I was well enough to go home was e-mail my father. It read: Thanks, old warrior. You were right about Bruno Schneider. What a strange man—mean, deceitful? He's dead at last, though I must admit his death gives me no great pleasure. But, I'm alive and hope the knowledge of this puts your mind at ease," David.

I didn't mention what happened to Ilse. Maybe, it was payback for the years he corresponded from places somewhere between the stars and the long ago. Maybe, it was too painful for me to share. In any case, being without the person I wanted most was what I was left with.

I took a can of soup out of a cabinet, had it half-opened, when the phone rang. It was Rosalie. She said she read an article about me in the *New York Times.* Seemed one of us had to be impressed just a little. She asked if I was all right. I said I was.

"I was sorry to hear about the woman who was killed."

"Ilse Van Ness. You knew her name, didn't you?"

"Yes."

"Don't play games, Rosalie."

"I was only trying to help."

"I'm afraid I wouldn't be very good company."

"And, here I was thinking you'd cheer me up."

"Would you like to see my collection of old newspapers and empty liquor glasses?"

"How about coming over to my place?"

"What are you collecting?"

"Better memories I hope."

"Chances are I'll talk mostly about her."

"I'd expect you would. Was she your one true love?"

"I'm sorry. I can't..." I broke in, leaning toward the liquor cabinet.

"Don't be sorry."

"I'm a little edgy. You've been very nice..."

"I'm a good listener."

"Tell me something?"

"Go on."

"Why do we twist our lives into so many knots?"

"So we have a chance to unravel them. Remember, we're the weavers of the future."

"Is that what we are?"

There was a moment of silence, broken when Rosalie said: "I'd like to make dinner for you. I can't imagine you having any desire to cook after what you've been through."

I remembered something Ilse said. "Do you think all women are paralyzed in the kitchen?" It brought an unexpected smile. I looked over my shoulder at the half-opened can of soup and asked, "Where did you say you lived?"

The End

About the Author

Ken Markel is a graduate of New York University and former editor at Magazine Management, a pulp fiction company publishing adventure magazines. His short stories have appeared in *True, Adventure Life, Sportsman,* and *Mystery Tales,* among others. Markel's fiction and poetry can be read in *The American Bard, The Berkshire Review,* and the *South Shore News.* His play, *The American Way,* was performed under the direction of Lee Strasberg.

Ken Markel holds a Master of Arts Degree from Queens College in Creative Writing. His thesis, *Last Train to Munich,* is the story of a German family and their struggle to survive the 1923 inflation…when paper money was less valuable to the starving population than a bartered egg.